UNDERCOVER LOVER SERIES

ZACK

UNDERCOVER LOVER SERIES

C. A. SALO

CHAPTER 1

SYDNEY GLANCED UP FROM her work as she heard the whining voice she knew so well, and with an inner shudder watched as the long legged, bleach blonde with a tight mini skirt, and fire engine red lipstick sat on the corner of her desk. "What do you want, Lori?" She leaned back on her chair with a sigh.

"Why is it you always ask me that when I come to see you?" Lori replied as she picked her teeth with a fingernail. "Can't I just stop in to say hi?"

Rolling her eyes, Sydney sighed, as her sister sucked on her finger. "Lori, we both know you don't just stop in to say hi." Sydney massaged her temple.

Lori jumped off the desk. "Fine. I wanted to know if you could spot me a twenty until Friday?" She picked up the stapler.

Sydney took out of her hand. "We've had this conversation before. The answer is no."

"Why not?"

"Because I'm not giving you money so you can go buy drugs." Sydney hissed under her breath.

"Give me a break, Syd; maybe I need it for food."

"Where did your food stamps go?"

"What is this? Twenty freaking questions?" Lori barked.

"What does it matter? All I'm asking for is a twenty; can't you even help me out? I'm your sister for Christ's sake, and it's not like you don't make enough to spare."

Oh yeah, same old argument, "How much I make is not the question. What did you do with the check you received last week?"

"That's not your business," Lori hissed. "What I do with my money is my affair."

"Then don't make it mine." God, she was sick of this crap. every two weeks, they had the same argument. "If you can't keep enough to pay your bills and your drug habit then get a job." Sydney snapped. She grabbed the arms of her chair in anger, so she didn't smack Lori upside the head.

"You're a bitch." Lori called out as she turned, heading down the hallway.

"I've been called worse." Sydney rose out of her chair.

"See if I ask you for anything again," Lori yelled down the hallway.

Sydney looked down at her watch, then back up at her sister. "Same time, two weeks from *now?*"

Lori stepped into the elevator and pushed the button. She glared at her sister and yelled,

"And you wonder why no man wants you, you prudie, overweight, mousy bitch? Fuck you."

Sydney sank back down onto her chair as the elevator doors closed, her hands coming up to cover her face as she her elbows rested on her desk.

"You okay, Syd?"

Sydney looked up at her boss, the assistant district attorney, Tamara Wong.

"Yeah, I just hate it when she comes in." She leaned back in her chair. "Talk about a stressful situation."

"Have you told her not to bother you during work hours?"

"Yes, but we all know how well that works."

"I can have the guards stop her at the doors."

"I know-if she doesn't stop I may just end up doing that."

"If there's anything I can do, let me know."

Sydney snorted, "How about a new sister?"

Tamara chuckled. "Sorry. We can choose our friends and we can choose our lovers, but relatives...well, we're stuck with them for the long haul."

"I know, I know." Sydney started when the phone rang. She held up her index finger to Tamara as she answered the phone. "Assistant D.A. Wong's office, how may I help you?" She waited and listened. "Yes sir, right away." She hung up the phone. "The D.A. would like to see you in his office, as in yesterday. His exact words."

"Did he say what about?"

"No. Only that ASAP came out of his mouth."

"Right. Well, why don't you go to lunch and I'll see you when I get back."

"Sure, do you want anything?" Sydney removed her purse from the drawer.

"No, I'm fine. Thanks," Tamara said, as she walked down the hallway.

~~*~~

Across town, Lori walked into the Mer-Fay bar. Mac's eyes narrowed at the new patron.

"Are you Mac?"

Smiling, he leaned an elbow on the counter. God, he hated when the junkies came in, especially the women. *See what she has and get rid of her fast*—that was his motto. "And who are you, sweet cheeks?" he asked, his gaze going from her red lipstick to her bleached hair and tight clothes. It took all his strength not to shudder.

Lori smiled at him. "I am the person who is going to make your day."

Mac chuckled. "And just how are you going to do that?"

"You're hot."

"Thank you. Is that how you plan on making my day? Or do you have something better?"

"No, I have something I think you, and some of your associates might find interesting."

"Something besides yourself?" *God, can I puke now, please?* When she smiled at him, he held back the wince that took over his mind, at the sight of her rotten teeth.

"Well of course, darling." Lori chuckled as she sat on the bar stool next to him.

Yeah, you keep thinking that. "Well, spit it out, honey. Time's money and you're wasting mine."

"Right, now let's talk about that money part. I want two hundred."

Mac laughed out loud. "You want, huh? What about I see what you have first and then we talk." His gaze followed her hand up to her breasts, not because she turned him on, because he didn't trust anyone. His brow arched when she pulled an audiotape out of her bra.

"This has some important information on it. Now about the money."

"Sweet Cheeks, I'm not giving you a red cent until I find out what is on this."

"You're right. Here, listen to it." She handed him the tape cassette. "I'll be waiting right here."

Mac took the tape between two fingers as he got off the bar stool, and smiled at her as he walked to the back of the bar and up a set of stairs. After listening to the recording, he picked up his cell phone and dialed. "It's Mac. We have a problem."

Walking back down the stairs, he saw the woman. She was still where he'd left her.

"Where did you get that?" he asked as he stood off to her side.

"Does it matter?" She smiled.

"Yes, it does. I have to make sure it's the real thing."

"Oh, it's real all right." Lori thrust her breasts out.

"Where did you get it?"

"Off the D.A.'s desk," she smiled. "I went in to see my stupid, fat sister, and as I was walking by the office I heard them playing this-so on my way out, I helped myself."

Mac's brows went up. "Your sister works for the D.A.?" he asked for clarification.

"No, she works for the Assistant D.A., and they deserve each other—prudish bitches,"

Lori sneered.

"How often do you see your sister?"

"Why does it matter? Are you going to pay me or not?"

Mac grabbed his wallet out of his back pocket. Opening it, he pulled out a hundred dollar bill. "It matters, because if you hear anything again, I want to know."

Lori took the money without counting. "Maybe we could go somewhere quiet."

Mac smiled at her. "I don't think so; I don't do druggies." He walked away.

"Hey, you gypped me," she yelled and ran after him, but he was already out of the parking lot on his bike.

~~*~~

Sydney gathered her purse before walking over to Tamara's office. Knocking on the door lightly with her knuckles, she waited until Tamara looked up. "I'm getting ready to leave; is there anything you need?"

"No, Sydney. I'm fine."

"Are you sure? Ever since I came back from lunch, you've been tense."

Tamara smiled. "I'm fine, just a case the D.A. wants my help with."

Sydney smiled. "Well, don't let it stress you out too much. Go home and jump in that Jacuzzi of yours with the jets on high."

"I think I may do just that. Are you walking home again?"

"Yeah, good for the body."

"Would you like a ride home?"

"Nah, I have to get my exercise somehow." Sydney chuckled.

"Syd, don't let what Lori said upset you. There is nothing wrong with you or the way you look."

"I know, but it still hurts. Well, I better get going before it gets dark. See you in the morning." She waved and turned from the door.

~~*~~

Sydney hadn't realized how dark it had gotten. She had stopped in at the small mom and pop store on the corner to get a few groceries for tonight's dinner, and when she came out it was dark. Holding her small bag, she walked with purpose down the street. It wasn't that this was a bad area, but you never knew what could happen, and she had left her mace at the apartment this morning by accident when she changed purses. After figuring out what had taken her so long, she swore. "Damn Lori," she mumbled to herself, realizing that instead of picking out what she needed and leaving she had stood in the aisles longer, hearing Lori's mean words in her head. She was still contemplating it when a motorcycle came up beside her.

"Get on," came a masculine voice.

Stunned, Sydney looked over at the man on the bike and stopped walking as he stopped right beside her. "Excuse me?"

"Get on." He looked straight at her with very green eyes.

"I- I don't think so," she stuttered, and started walking down the street again. Sydney's heart sped up, palms damp as he followed her. She wanted to know why there was never a cop around when you needed one. Taking a deep breath, Sydney realized that it was up to her to get rid of him. She stopped turning to look right at him, watching as he stopped the bike.

"Listen buddy, I'm not a hooker. You have to go to the West side for that, so leave me alone."

"Lady!" The man yelled over the engine of his bike as he came up beside her again.

"Listen..." she started.

"No, you listen. Don't look, but there's a guy following you. When I was stopped at the light, I saw him come out of the alley. He's been following you for three blocks, so get on."

Sydney's mouth opened and shut, not sure what to say. She couldn't tell if he was telling the truth, so she glanced down the street and saw a guy dressed in jeans and a leather jacket, leaning against a light post, staring her way.

"Damn it, I said not to look," he hissed.

Sydney whipped her eyes back to him, frightened as hell now. "Well, how am I supposed to know if you're telling the truth or not?"

"Just get on. Here he comes."

Sydney glanced down the sidewalk again, her eyes widened as the man walked toward them.

"Lady, come on."

Sydney turned to the man, speechless; she didn't know what the hell to do, until the guy on the sidewalk spoke.

"Hey sweetie, if I knew you had services to sell..."

Sydney's lips parted on a gasp as he started withdrawing a knife.

"Jesus, lady, let's go!" The man on the bike yanked on her arm.

Sydney realized she dropped the bag she was carrying, but everything seemed to be happening in slow motion. She didn't even remember getting on the back of the bike until she heard him tell her to hang on. And she did, wrapping both arms around his waist. She left no inch of space between them.

When she noticed they weren't moving, she opened her eyes and saw him looking back at her. "You all right?" he asked.

"Y-yes," she answered. "Why are we stopped?"

"Red light, sweetheart, but don't worry. He's too far behind us."

"Oh, okay, are you taking me home?"

"I will in a bit; I have an appointment to get to first," he replied as he started the bike rolling when the light turned green.

"B-but I have to go home."

"And I have an appointment I can't miss. Don't worry sweetheart, I won't keep you out past your bedtime."

She opened her mouth to say something and shut it when he revved the engine as they drove down the road. Laying her cheek on his back, her eyes fluttered shut, letting the calm of the wind blowing around her take away the stress of the day. Of course, the smell of warm leather and masculine male wasn't bad either.

CHAPTER 2

SYDNEY FELT THE BIKE slow and then stop. She didn't budge an inch even after he shut the engine off.

Mac sat there for a second, waiting for her to move. Turning his head, he tried to see her over his shoulder. "Hey, lady?"

"Yes?" Sydney whispered.

"We're parked."

Her eyes fluttered open. "I know."

"You've never ridden on a bike before, huh?"

"Um, no. Why?"

Mac chuckled. "Because you still have a death grip on me."

Sydney released him a little too fast; going sideways, she thought for sure she was going to end up on the ground until a strong grip grabbed her arm, setting her straight.

"Easy honey, it's all right."

Sydney blushed. "I'm sorry."

"Don't be. It's not every day I get held like that," he smiled. Sydney glanced up at him. He was a good-looking man; she hadn't noticed that when he pulled her onto his bike. He smiled, and the heat rushed to her cheeks. She had just been caught staring. Lowering her eyes, she tried to think of something to say, but of course nothing would come to mind. She didn't talk to men except at work, and it was always about work. She looked up when he got off the bike.

Mac held his hand out so he could help her off. Sydney slowly slid her palm over his calloused one. Still holding her hand in his, he started walking for the door.

Sydney stopped when she looked up, causing Mac to stop mid-stride and turn to look at her.

"Isn't this the um, rough side of town?" she asked, as the smile reappeared on his face.

"It's not that rough."

"Are you sure I should go in there?" She eyed the bar.

Mac's eyebrow went up. "And you're suggesting that I should leave you out here alone?"

Sydney's eyes widened. "No. Can't you just take me home first?"

Mac glanced at his watch. "Sorry, sweet cheeks. Not enough time." He started walking with her to the door again.

Sydney glanced up at the sign. "Mer-fay," she said out loud. "What does that have to do with a bar?"

Mac turned and looked at her. "What do you mean?"

Sydney pushed her glasses up onto the bridge of her nose. "Well, mer-fay means -sea-fairy. It's an old saying from the sailors, it means mermaid."

Mac smiled at her, "And how do you know that?"

"I like mythological things and read a lot."

"And do you believe in mermaids?"

"Well, there is truth to every myth." She lowered her eyes. Great, now he was thinking she had no social life and she was a quack.

Mac chuckled. "So right you are." He opened the door to the bar.

Sydney tried to see ahead of them, but it was difficult with his broad shoulders in her way and the fact that he had to be at least six feet to her five feet three. Sydney slid a glance to her right and quickly turned her gaze to stare at his back. What kind of business did he have in a bar like this? Sydney gripped his hand tighter when a few of the men issued some suggestive comments her way. Sydney liked how he tightened his hold to reassure her and glanced up when he stopped. He shot the guys a look, bringing their comments to an end and walked when he did until they reached the end of the bar.

"Ooh." Sydney gasped when his hands wrapped around her waist, lifting her in front of him to sit on the barstool.

"Walt," he called out.

Sydney studied his profile, his gaze meeting hers as the bartender came over to them.

"Watch her for me," he said, and then turned to walk away.

Sydney grabbed his hand back into hers.

"It's all right. I'll be right over there," Mac pointed to a small table in an alcove where a man already sat. "Walt's right here, don't worry." He squeezed her hand before turning.

"Hey, Sugar, what's your poison?" Walt asked.

Her brows drew together.

"Drink, doll. What do you want to drink?" he smiled.

"Oh. Um, Coke, please."

"Straight or something with it?"

"Just Coke, thank you." Sydney turned her head when she sensed someone looking at her and came face to face with one of the men who had made some of the cat calls when she'd walked into the bar. Turning away, Sydney lifted her glass, sipping the cold sweet cola as he continued to stare. He was skinny, not bulked up like the rest of these guys, but not harmless either.

"Hey, baby. What's your name?"

Sydney sat there and ignored the man, hoping he'd give up and go away.

"Hey, I asked what your name is. Didn't you hear me?"

"Yes, and I would like it if you left me alone," she answered, without looking at him.

"Hey, that's rude."

"So were the comments coming out of your mouth when I walked in, so bug off." No matter what she said, the guy would not leave her alone. When he grabbed her arm she whipped her head around, yanked her arm and pushed him back. "Do not touch me!"

"Mac!" Walt bellowed.

Mac looked up. "Greeley!" He shouted.

Sydney backed up to the bar as the man, Greeley stepped away.

"Whom did she come in with?" Mac asked with authority.

"You."

"That's right, so leave her alone. Now." Mac ordered.

Sydney moved her gaze to Mac as the other man walked away. My God, he was huge. She knew he was built well from having her arms wrapped around him on the bike, but oh my. he had to be at least six-foot three, with shoulder length wavy brown hair. His white t-shirt, black biker jacket, and form-fitting jeans could not hide that fact. Her gaze moved slowly back toward his face. Her nipples strained against her bra as she took in the neatly trimmed beard and mustache before she met his gaze and looked straight into those green eyes. Her face heated when he winked at her with a smile as he sat back down, giving his attention once more to the other man sitting at the table.

"Don't worry, doll. No one in here will give you a real hassle."

Turning her head when she heard the crack of pool balls, Sydney watched with interest as the game ensued. It really wasn't a fair game. She doubted the loser played very much, so she turned to Walt. "Do you think they'd mind if I went over to watch?"

"Nah, they're pretty good guys and they know you came in with Mac."

Getting up, she made her way over to the pool table and observed as the man who was losing prepared to take a shot. She never could hide what she was thinking very well and when the obvious winner spoke, her chest rose with a deep breath.

"You think you could do better?" the man asked with curiosity and a smile.

"W-well, yes, I mean you only have one ball left to sink and if he misses the shot, then you win."

"Think you can do better, darling?" the loser, Nick asked.

Sydney looked over at the man. "Yes. Not to o-offend you," she said, as she looked back to the other man.

"Give her your stick, Nick. Let's see what Mac's lady can do."

Sydney wasn't about to argue with them on being anyone's lady, especially if Mac protected her. She took the pool stick that was handed to her, and sighted it for curves as she inhaled deeply, trying to calm herself.

"Good luck," Nick said, and backed off.

"Thank you." Sydney set the stick against the pool table

for a minute as she took off her jacket and purse, placing them on a stool. Picking the stick back up, she grabbed the chalk and cubed the tip before sighting the table again. Taking the stick, she pointed to the far right side pocket.

Five," she said, and then pointed to the left middle pocket. "Seven." Sydney bent over as she lined up the shot and watched as the balls went where she said they would. After sinking every ball but one, she glanced up to see a crowd had gathered. Even Walt was standing by with Mac beside him. Looking back at the table, she sighted up her next shot.

"Honey, there is no way you're going to make that shot." Brian smiled.

Sydney looked up at her opponent as he grinned when several people standing by agreed with him.

"Want to make a bet?" he asked with a smile.

"That wouldn't be fair," she replied as she took aim. "For you." She hit the ball and watched as it went into the pocket she'd designated for it.

Sydney put the stick on the table. "Thank you; that was a good game." She picked up her items and headed over to where Walt and Mac had moved back by the bar.

Glancing down at her, Mac liked the way her ivory colored silk tank clung to her chest.

"Good game."

"Thank you."

"Ready to get going?"

"Yes, but could you tell me where the ladies' room is first?"

Taking a hold of her hand, Mac smiled. "Sure, honey." He started walking toward the staircase.

Sydney followed him. "The bathrooms are upstairs?"

"Mine is," he answered, as they walked down a hallway until they reached a door on the right. Opening it, he moved out of the way and motioned for her to go in.

"Yours?" She walked into the apartment.

"Yeah, I'd rather you use this one. We don't get many women of reputable character in here, and I'm not sure if Walt cleaned the ladies' room downstairs."

Sydney looked around the huge apartment. It looked like it ran the length of the entire building. "You live here?" she asked, as he closed the door.

"Yeah," he answered, as he headed across the room. "This way."

Sydney followed him, and when passing an open door on the left she looked in and saw a king-size bed still rumpled from use. She glanced away when he turned.

"Light switch is on the left." He said, walking back into the living room.

Sydney was washing her hands when she caught her image in the mirror and winced. Some tendrils had come out of her hair clip and swayed around her face. Bringing up her hands, she tucked them behind her ears, but that only looked worse. Undoing the clip, she let her hair fall and after running her fingers through it, gathered it back up again, securing the clip in place. Opening the door, she shut the light off and walked back to the living room.

"Would you like something to drink before we go?" Mac asked.

Sydney turned toward the small kitchen area. "No, thank you."

"All right."

"Mac?"

"Yeah." He put his jacket back on.

"You- you weren't doing anything illegal, w-were you?" she asked, meeting his gaze.

"No, why?"

"Well, because I'd have to turn you in, if you were."

"You a cop?" he asked in a low voice.

"No, but I do work for the D.A.'s office."

"Why would you think I was doing something illegal?" He walked up to her, mentally giving her credit for not backing down from his six-foot three-inch frame.

"B-because, you met that man here and it's not the most…"

"Sweetheart," he said. "I met him here because I own this place, and he is one of my local beer distributors."

"Oh, I'm sorry then." Her cheeks were getting hot. "You were nice enough to help me and I judged you b-because of appearances."

"Would you really turn me in?"

"Yes."

Mac smiled. "Well I can't blame you for being judgmental, especially after Greeley. He does that to people, but he's harmless."

"I enjoyed the game of pool. I'm not a bar person, so I shouldn't be judging the people in them."

"Then where did you learn how to shoot?"

"The Billiard's Room. Every third Thursday the library brings the teenagers down to play."

"Interesting. Well, then I guess I should get you home." He smiled, taking her hand in his.

Sydney waved to Walt as they walked by, the heat from outside hitting her as they went through the door.

"Where do you live?"

"On the East side. Grayson Street."

"No problem, I know where that is." Mac glanced down at her. "Are you getting on?" he asked when she just stood there.

"Don't you have a car or something?"

"Nope," he said. "What's your name? It doesn't seem right calling you 'lady' all the time."

"Oh, it's Sydney. Sydney Ripley."

"Like Sydney, Australia."

"Exactly like—that's what I was named after," she answered and started lifting her leg, stopping when her skirt stopped her. Lowering her hands, she started hiking it up. Glancing up she noticed Mac's eyes on her legs.

"Could you turn the other way please?" Sydney asked.

His lips turned up into a cocky smile as he followed her request and sat on the bike. "Sorry honey, you have nice legs. Why did your parents name you after a city?"

"Because that's where I was conceived." She wrapped her arms around his waist.

"Well, how about that," he stated with a smile as he started his bike.

"Is this a Harley?" Sydney asked, as they started out of the parking lot.

"Yeah, why?"

"It's kind of loud, isn't it?"

"That, Sydney, is one of the joys of owning a Harley," he answered, as they took off down the road.

At the second stop light he turned his head to look at her over his shoulder. "Are you cold or just shaking because of the bike?"

"A little cold." She let go when he started taking his jacket off.

Mac handed it to her and watched as she put it on.

Wrapping the warm insides of the jacket around her, Sydney smiled. "Thank you." She saw that drop-dead gorgeous smile appear on his face, and then watched it disappeared as his eyes went to the vehicle that just pulled up beside them. Sydney turned to see a patrol car, and quickly turned away, pressing her cheek onto his warm back, when she saw who was driving.

"Don't like cops either, huh?" he asked, as he moved his hand to her bare thigh.

"No, that's not it," she whispered.

"Syd, is that you?" one of the officers asked.

Sydney turned her head and smiled at the officer driving. "Hi, John." She cringed when his gaze went from her to Mac.

"Syd, what the hell are you doing?"

"Getting a ride home."

John looked at the man driving the bike. "Don't I know you?" he asked, as Mac turned to look at the car.

"No, officer. You don't."

"I've seen you somewhere. Pull over, I'll take her home."

"John, I'm fine; he helped me. Some guy was following me from work and had a knife. He helped me."

John looked back at the man. "I know I've seen you somewhere."

"Probably, officer. But I haven't done anything wrong," Mac replied, as the other officer in the car whispered to John.

"Hi, Barney." Sydney knew if anyone could talk John into leaving her alone, it was his partner.

"Hey Syd, you sure you'll be all right?" Barney asked.

"Yes."

"Fine by me. John, leave her alone."

John narrowed his eyes at Mac. "I'll be checking to make sure she's at work tomorrow—safe. Got it?"

Mac smiled sarcastically. "Yes sir, Mr. Police Officer, sir." He moved his fingers over the bare skin of her thigh and grinned as the patrolman's eyes widened.

"Mac, you shouldn't do that," she whispered, as he turned to look at her.

"Want to freak him out?" he asked, just before he brought his hand up off her thigh and around the back of her neck, pulling her down to him for a kiss.

Sydney closed her eyes as his lips touched hers. They were gentle and firm at the same time, and tasted like spearmint. When she felt cool air, her eyes fluttered open and saw his smile.

"Hold on." He turned back around as he drove through the green light. Sydney caught the surprised look on John's face as they went past him, and hid her smile behind the collar of Mac's jacket, noticing the cruiser wasn't following the bike as they came to a stop at the next light.

"Ex-boyfriend?" Mac asked, without turning to look at her.

"No worse, he's my cousin."

"Wonderful."

Sydney gave him the directions to her apartment as they drove onto her street. He parked the bike in front of her door and helped her off. Sydney opened her purse and took her keys out as they walked up the small sidewalk.

"I thought you said you lived in an apartment?" He asked as they stood in front of a duplex town house.

"It is an apartment." She opened the door.

"Looks more like a condo to me."

20

"If I could afford to buy a condo, I'd have a house," she answered, as she turned to look at him. "Thank you for helping me tonight."

Mac met her gaze. "No problem, honey. Just watch your surroundings next time."

"I usually do, but I had a lot on my mind today."

"Work?"

"No, family." She smiled.

"Hmm, yeah, family will do it to you every time. Stay off dark streets. Next time I may not be there to help."

"I will."

"You know, you're a pretty good pool player."

"Thank you."

"Anytime you want to play, I'm there after six."

"Okay, is that an invitation?" she asked with a smile.

"It is," Mac replied. "I'd like to play you one-on-one."

"That's good, because I don't do teams," Sydney replied. Her cheeks heated up as she caught on to the double meaning. "Oh," she whispered when he grinned.

Mac chuckled. "Me either."

"Oh, your jacket." Sydney blushed as she took it off and handed it back.

"Thanks," he said as he put it back on. Bringing his hand up, Mac cupped her chin.

Sydney met his gaze. Her chest rose, hardened nipples brushing against her bra as his eyes moved to her lips. *Oh, please.*

Damn, he wanted nothing more than to put her up against the wall and attack those luscious lips. "Remember what I said: stay off dark streets."

Sydney waited; she wanted him to kiss her again so badly. And then his hand left her and cool air hit her warm skin, her gaze on him as he walked back to his bike and straddle it. After rolling it back, he started it up and lifted his hand to her as he took off. Sydney gulped for air; she hadn't realized that she had been holding her breath. Turning, she walked into her apartment and locked the door before putting her purse on the hallway table. Looking up, she caught herself in the mirror. "No wonder he didn't kiss you. What a mess." She said, as she removed the clip and massaged her head as she walked to her bathroom.

When Mac rolled to a stop at a red light he pulled his cell phone out of the inner pocket of his jacket. Dialing, he waited for someone to answer. "It's Mac. I made contact."

"How'd it go?"

"I just dropped her off. We may have another problem. Her cousin's a cop. He pulled up alongside of us, thought he recognized me."

"Car number?"

"One-eighteen."

"What happened?"

"They tailed us to her place and they're following me now. Take care of it."

"I will. Don't get your panties in a bunch."

"Fine, later." Mac said, as he finished and pushed the end button, putting the cell phone back into his pocket, before taking off down the road. Mac glanced in his rearview mirror as the patrol car followed him. After about a mile, they turned off, heading back toward town. "Stupid shits." He continued his way down to the waterfront, picking up the pace to make his appointment. The people he was meeting with did not like tardiness for any reason.

"Unless you're dead," he mumbled as he turned onto the pier.

CHAPTER 3

TAMARA WALKED UP AND stopped in front of Sydney's desk. "Okay girl, spill your guts."

Sydney looked up at her with a smile. "What?"

"You know what. You've been on cloud nine since you walked in here this morning." Tamara scooted to the side and sat on the corner of Sydney's desk.

"Well, I met a man last night." She proceeded to tell Tamara the story.

"I think you should take him up on his offer and go down to play some pool."

"Do you think it was an offer, or was he just being nice?" Sydney questioned.

"I think it was an attempt to see you again."

"Yeah, but he didn't kiss me after he dropped me off."

"So he kissed you before, didn't he?" Tamara asked.

"That was only to freak John out."

"Maybe that was just an excuse. You did say that he had his hand on your leg before he kissed you."

"Yeah, but oh, I don't know. I mean, I don't even have any clothes to wear."

"Just put on a pair of jeans and a t-shirt, grab your pool stick and go." Tamara said.

~~*~~

Sydney looked up from paperwork when someone stopped in front of her desk, and she smiled when she saw her cousin. "Hi, John."

"Sydney, I see you made it home all right last night."

"Of course, I did. I told you I was fine." She laid her hands on top of the desk as he nodded his head.

"It's a good thing he didn't try kissing you again," John blurted out.

"You followed us home, didn't you?" She stood up, her hands balling into fists at her sides. "Didn't you?" she hissed.

"I plead the fifth."

"Damn you, John Monroe. I'm a big girl! I don't need you following me home; I don't need you protecting me anymore."

"That's not what you said last night. You said someone was following you with a knife."

"And I'm fine," she barked.

"Yeah, because some long-haired freak on a Harley helped you," he retorted, his voice rising with his own anger.

Sydney brought her hand up and pointed at him. "He is not a freak. Don't you dare talk bad about him. Do you hear me?"

"Or what?" he yelled back.

"Or you'll take that badge off and I'll meet you outside."

"I'm not ten anymore, Syd. You couldn't kick my ass if you tried."

"Catch me outside. How 'bout that?"

"What is all this yelling about?" Tamara asked, as she walked out of her office.

"I'm getting ready to kick my cousin's ass," Sydney said, her gaze not wavering under John's intense stare.

"There is going to be no ass-kicking on my time." Tamara stood in the middle of them.

"Then tell him I don't need a watch dog. He followed me home last night." Sydney said through clenched teeth.

"Tell her to stop hanging out with long-haired bikers."

"I'll hang out with whomever I damn well please."

"Why? Because he showed you some attention? Jesus, Syd, you don't hook up with that type of guy just because you're desperate!" John spouted.

Her eyes started tearing up.

"Syd, I'm sorry."

"You're a jerk," she said, before rushing by him to the ladies' room.

"Syd, I'm sorry."

~~*~~

Sydney was quiet for the rest of the day, not talking unless she had to.

Tamara looked at her with sad eyes. "Sydney, don't listen to him."

Sydney looked up at her with red-rimmed eyes. "Why not, it's true isn't it? It's not like I have men falling at my feet. I'm not the kind of woman men ask out for no reason. I guess drugs weren't affecting Lori that much, were they? I mean if my cop of a cousin notices it, then why not my drug addict of a sister?" Taking a deep breath, Sydney let it out slowly, trying to hold back the pain ramming her chest from the inside. No one understood how she felt; no one ever understood.

"I've had sex once, Tam, and it wasn't even good. Would you like to know why? Because I can tell you, it was a dare. When I was in college, I was still a virgin and a fraternity found out and dared one of its members that he couldn't do me." Breathing deeply, her body shook as she continued. "I thought he liked me because he spent so much time with me; we saw each other for four months before we had sex. Then as soon as it was over, he jumped off me laughing, and spilled out why he'd done it, calling me a stupid, ugly- looking geek, and that Lori was right, that I was a terrible screw."

Sydney reached over and grabbed tissue, bringing it up to her face to catch the tears. "You see, she set me up. My own sister set up the dare; she even rewarded the winner a blow job and John knows it. He found out later that night. The guy was bragging about it at a local bar and John overheard everything. He beat the shit out of the guy." she sadly chuckled out the last.

"John is protective of you, Sydney. That much is a fact. But he should back off and let you grow up, let you live."

"Easier said than done."

"Come on, Sydney. Let's go see if my stylist can get you in."

"What do you mean?"

"You have beautiful hair. Let's see what can be done with it."

~~*~~

Tamara leaned over the chair and met Sydney's gaze in the mirror. "See? I told you you're a swan."

Sydney chuckled.

"I'm serious. You have gorgeous hair, Syd. You should wear it down more often," Tamara replied as she looked at Sydney's waist-length hair. "And men love long hair." She wiggled her eyebrows.

Sydney chuckled. "I thought makeup would just make me look like Lori." Sydney eyed herself in the mirror.

"That's because she wears it like a hooker," Tamara replied. "This looks absolutely natural. Think you can do it at home?"

"Yes."

"Good, I'm starving. Let's go get something to eat."

Sydney and Tamara walked out of the salon laughing, with no idea they were being watched and followed.

~~*~~

Sydney felt great the next day, as she walked down the steps of the courthouse. Everyone who came in had commented on her new look. She smiled, as she remembered one of the lawyers who had come in. He'd almost tripped as he followed Tamara to her office, because he tried looking back to catch another glance of her. Sydney turned her head when she heard a bike coming up from behind her; smiling, she stopped and waited.

"I wasn't sure that was you," Mac replied, as his eyes moved over her. She still wore the skirt suit. This time it was lavender, but she had on a very light layer of makeup and her hair was down, pulled back at the sides. Damn if his cock didn't go hard.

"Hi, Mac. What are you up to?" Sydney asked, as he took off his sunglasses.

"I had some errands in town and was coming by to see if you wanted to go grab something to eat."

Sydney smiled at him. "I'd love to."

"Good, jump on." He held out his hand to help.

Sydney reached down and hiked her skirt up a little before taking his hand and seating herself behind him.

"Still have that death grip, huh?" he asked when she wrapped her arms around him.

"Yeah."

"That's all right, honey. I don't mind." He smiled before turning around. Slowly taking off from the curb, he drove to a small fish shack down on the wharf.

~~*~~

"This is the best fish I've ever had. Where did you find this place?" Sydney asked.

Mac smiled as she picked up a piece of fillet and popped it in her mouth. "My dad used to bring me here all the time." He watched her pop a finger in her mouth to clean off the breadcrumbs; his body hardened at the mere sight of her lips wrapped around her finger, sucking. When she went to put another one in her mouth he lifted his hand and placed it over hers, lowering both down to the table. "Honey, don't do that."

Sydney was startled at first, her gaze shooting to his. "I'm sorry, that was rude of me." She lowered her gaze to the table.

Mac realized she thought he was criticizing her. "It wasn't that honey, it was making me horny." He grinned, as she lifted eyes filled with surprise to meet his; holding her gaze for a few moments, Mac leaned over the small table, pressing his lips to hers with a soft kiss. Sydney sighed as his lips met hers several more times.

"Hey, I see no *kissy, kissy* on my menu."

Mac smiled against Sydney's lips before sitting back on his chair. "Sydney, meet the owner of the fish shack, Lei Min. Lei Min, this is Sydney."

Sydney straightened up as a petite woman walked toward them.

"Mac, you finally bring pretty woman to eat here and you get the *kissy, kissy* on. No *kissy, kissy*! You eat, and who are you calling my fine establishment a shack?"

"Lei, you named it the Fish Shack." he snickered.

"Ya, ya Mac, you eat fish, give good strength for night time nookie-nookie," she laughed as she walked away.

Mac chuckled and stood up. "You ready to leave?"

"Yes, of course." Sydney wiped her fingers on the paper napkin and then started gathering up the paper plates their food had come on.

Mac grabbed their drinks and followed her over to the trash bin. His eyes on her bottom, he smiled. After throwing the trash away, he put his hand at the small of her back and escorted her back to his bike. Holding her hand, his eyes lowered as she hiked her skirt up just enough with her other hand to seat herself on the bike. "You know, you look great in skirts, but a newer, slimmer style would look even better on you." He straddled his bike.

"Oh yeah, and what would you know of women's clothes?"

"Nothing, but your legs in a pencil skirt." Mac smiled as he growled. "Or something above the knee would show'em off."

"Hmmm, so you're a leg man." She smiled.

His lips turned up into a grin.

"Legs and butt baby, legs and butt."

"I'll keep that in mind." Sydney met his gaze; she loved how the gold flecks swam around in them. She leaned in meeting him halfway. The soft brush of his lips had tingles streaming from the back of her head down her spine.

"Ready?" he asked against her lips, then backed up and put his sunglasses on.

"Yes." Sydney put her arms around him.

Mac smiled and patted her hands with one of his as he turned the key and pulled out onto the road.

"W-where are we going?" she asked over the roar of the engine, when she noticed they weren't heading to her house.

"Someplace pretty." He looked back over his shoulder with a smile, his hand moving to lie against her bare thigh.

Sydney smiled and laid her cheek against his shoulder as they continued down the road. When they started slowing down, she lifted her head and watched as he pulled the bike up close to a guardrail in a park on the Westside. After he shut the engine off, he took off his sunglasses and stood, getting off the bike. Mac turned around and sat back on it, facing her.

"What are you doing?" Sydney asked with a smile.

"Getting ready to watch the sun set." He took her hands in his to hold as they observed the sun set together.

~~*~~

"That was beautiful. I haven't sat down to watch the sun set since I was little." She noticed the lasting shadows play with the contours of his face.

Mac brought his hands up and ran a finger along the curve of her jaw. "A beautiful sunset for a beautiful lady," leaning forward, brushing his lips across hers ever so slow.

Sydney leaned into the kiss, her hands moving to his shoulders as a soft sigh escaped.

Mac leisurely moved his lips over hers, pressing soft kisses across her bottom lip as his teeth nipped her lightly. Bringing his hands up, he placed them on her waist, lifting her closer to him, settling her with her thighs resting across his as he wrapped his arms around her.

Sydney gasped when she felt his erection rubbing against her mound, giving Mac the opening to slide his tongue along her bottom lip, before slipping inside to taste her more fully.

He could hear her breathing escalate and was about to deepen the kiss when a big spot of light hit them, causing them both to jump back and the bike to rock.

Sydney yelped and held onto Mac as he stopped the bike, grabbed her at the same time. "It's all right, it won't fall," he said, then turned his head toward the light. "What the hell do you want?"

Sydney turned her head toward the light, trying to block the glare with her hand.

"Syd, let's go," came an irritated male voice.

"John, is that you?" she asked.

"Of course, it's me. Let's go." He shut the light off and walked in front of the cruiser.

"Wonderful," Mac mumbled, as he lifted Sydney off him to stand on the ground and followed.

"John, what the hell do you think you're doing?" Sydney asked as she walked up to him.

"Keeping you out of trouble." He placed his hands on his utility belt.

"I told you to stop following me; I'm not a child."

"No, you're not. That's why I'm taking you home, especially after what I just saw."

"What you just saw was two consenting adults kissing. I'm not going anywhere with you, so get it out of your head right now!"

"Do you want him to use you, too?"

"John..." Sydney started, eyes widening when she realized where he was going with the conversation.

"Like that bastard in college..."

"John, don't..." her voice dropped.

"Because that's all men think you're good for..."

"John, please..."

"What, you think leaving your hair down and putting some makeup on is going to change that? They screw you and then laugh in your face not two seconds later."

"Jo-hn." her head slowly shook as tears gathered in her eyes.

"You're too damn easy, Syd. It doesn't matter what you do, men pick up on how desperate you are for their attention, particularly guys like that." His voice rose as he pointed to Mac. "Why in the hell do you think no man wants to go near you? Because they know what a leach for attention you'd be and guys don't want that; they want sex, even if they must put up with your desperate attempts until they get it."

Sydney looked at him as tears flowed down her face, a sob breaking from her throat as her heart stabbed a painful rhythm under her ribs.

"Christ, man, what's wrong with you?" Mac asked.

John lowered his voice. "Syd," he said, as a tear trailed down her cheek. "Come on, let me take you home."

"W-why, s-sooo y-you can s-say m-more m-m-mean things t-tooo m-me?" she asked, as he ran a hand over his face.

"I just don't want you to get hurt."

"W-what do you th-think you just d-did?"

"Look at him, for Pete's sake. He'll turn you into a Lori."

"I know what he looks like, John," she replied, some of the anger coming back.

"Then what the hell is wrong with you? Do you want to be like Lori?"

"Lori has nothing to do with this, and you leave him alone."

"Why? He's leaning on his bike over there not doing a damn thing!"

"Maybe because if I did, you'd find a reason to throw me in jail," Mac responded as he came to stand behind Sydney.

"What the hell is he supposed to do, John?!" Sydney yelled.

"Why don't you stop being so damn desperate for a man's attention."

Sydney saw red; balling her fist, she slugged him right in the eye, watching as he stumbled back and Mac's arms went around her, holding her arms down. "You're an asshole!" She cried, as Barney come around the side of the car.

John flung off Barney's hand as Mac held her. "This isn't over," he said, pointing at Mac before he turned on his heel and walked to the squad car. Sydney's chest heaved as the tires spun.

Mac turned her in his embrace, holding her to him as he ran his hands down the length of her hair. "Are you all right?" he whispered next to her ear.

"Yes, I'd like to go home, please." She mumbled against his chest.

"All right, come on." He took her hand in his and led her back to his bike, helping her on. Before he seated himself, he took off his jacket. "Here. The sun's down; it may get a little chilly."

Sydney looked up at him as she put the jacket on. "Thank you." She wrapped her arms around him as soon as he seated himself in front of her, sighing she lay her cheek on his back closing her eyes.

Mac parked the bike in front of her apartment and helped her off. Escorting her to the door, he waited for her to open it and to say something.

Sydney took off his jacket and handed it back to him, keeping her eyes lowered.

Mac put it on. "Are you coming down on Friday to play some pool?"

"Why?"

"Because I want to play against you." He smiled.

"N-no, I mean why would you want me to-after tonight?"

Mac saw confusion and fear enter her beautiful eyes. "Because I like you."

"B-but John…" she started, and he cut her off.

"Can go to hell," he said, bringing his fingers up to trail them gently down the side of her cheek. Leaning down, he pressed feather-light kisses on her lips. "Friday, after six," he murmured before kissing her again.

A burning heat unfurled within Sydney, leaving her weak-kneed as her eyes fluttered open to see his eyes fixed on her. "Are you sure?" she asked.

"For a round of pool? You bet," he replied, trying to lighten the mood of the night as he leaned in for another kiss. He loved the feel of her soft sensuous lips. "Can I ask a favor?" He met her gaze.

"What?"

"Leave your hair down."

"But it will get in my way. Have you ever tried to play

pool with hair in your face?" she asked, watching as the side of his mouth lifted in a smile.

"What do you think?"

Sydney smiled back. "Okay, this much hair then?" She pulled some around to lie over her shoulder.

Mac chuckled as he reached for some hair, letting it slide through his fingers. "I guess you've got me there. Okay, how about a ponytail?"

She shook her head. "Makes me look ten. How about just up and out of my face?"

"Hmm, all right. As long as you don't pull it back in a chignon."

"Deal." Sydney held out her hand for a shake. Mac lifted her hand with his and placed light kisses on the back of her knuckles. Sydney inhaled sharply, her gaze lowered, following his movement. Her pussy tightened with excitement.

Mac lowered her hand. "I'll see you on Friday, then."

"Y-yes, Friday, after six."

Mac smiled at her. "After six." His fingers slipped from hers as he walked away.

Lifting her hand, she returned his wave as he took off down the road.

CHAPTER 4

SYDNEY PARKED HER CAR in the parking lot in front of the bar and breathed deeply. Her eyes glanced at the clock in her car, 7:15. Breathing in through her nose and out through her mouth one last time, she shut the engine off and opened the door, bringing her pool stick case out with her. After locking and shutting the car, she started for the door. She could hear the strands of alternative rock music and loud male voices coming from within. Opening the door, she stepped inside and started toward the bar, looking for Mac. The place was crowded tonight and more than one catcall came her way.

"Hey baby, want to dance?"

"Forget it Mel, the lady is with me," Mac replied, as he came up behind the biker and held out his hand for her, which she didn't hesitate to take.

"Sorry Ma'am, didn't realize you're Mac's lady." He smiled as he stepped away.

Mac's eyes lowered, roaming over her body. "You look good in jeans and a t-shirt." He smiled, his hand tightening on hers as he turned.

"Thank you."

"How about something to drink?" he asked over his shoulder as they started for the end of the bar.

"Hey doll, heard you belted a cop," Walt said as he came up to them.

Sydney's eyes whipped to Mac, watching as he shrugged a shoulder. "He's my cousin." She returned her gaze to Walt.

"Still a cop, doll. What's your poison?"

Sydney was quick to catch on this time. "Coke with Captain's. please." Walt smiled as he went about getting her the drink. "There are more people tonight."

"Yeah, Friday, sorry."

"It's all right," she said and laid her case against the bar.

"You have your own pool stick?" He raised an eyebrow.

Sydney glanced up at him with a smile. "Still want to play against me?"

Mac leaned down, brushing his lips against hers as he kept her gaze. "You bet. Let me go put our names in at the table." He walked over to the chalkboard.

She'd have to beat three people before she'd be able to play him. Not a problem. Sydney smiled when she caught Mac's gaze on her as she took the two pieces of her pool stick out of its bag and put it together. Her nipples grazed the cotton bra as he bent down, settling his mouth over hers in a gentle but firm kiss. Her nostrils flared. The scent of leather and Old Spice ricocheted through her system, tingles shot out of her nerve endings and her bottom lip trembled as her eyes fluttered.

"Hey Sydney, you're up," Greeley called.

Sydney sat back, her gaze meeting Mac's. "I'm up."

"Yeah, so am I," he responded.

Her cheeks turned red as she walked to the pool table.

Mac grinned, his eyes on her bottom as he turned to Walt. "How many has she had?"

"Still on her first one."

Mac looked down to see that her glass was still half full. "Strengthen it up and keep them coming until I say so."

Walt stared at him. "Sure you want to do that?"

"Don't question me, Walt. I just need her loose enough to talk."

"You're the boss." He reached for the bottle of Captain's, pouring it into her glass until it was full.

~~*~~

Sydney and Mac were halfway through their game when he glanced over at her. He could tell she was feeling the effects of the alcohol. "How ya doing, honey?"

"Fine, why? Want to quit?" she asked over the table as she took another sip of her drink. "Mac, how many of these have I had?"

"I'm not sure. Why? You feel all right?"

"Yeah, just a little buzz, but I'm positive this is still my first drink." Sydney smiled as she lined up her shot; she missed as she missed the looks the other men around the pool table shot Mac.

Mac kept his eye on her, even as he took over the table winning the game. After he sank the last ball he walked over, putting his hands on her waist. "You all right?" he asked as he looked down at her.

"Yeah, but I need to go to the bathroom."

"Okay honey," he said, his eyes moving to Greeley. "Take our names off the board, will you." Greeley nodded. Turning her slowly, his hands on her hips, he helped her upstairs to his apartment. "Do you remember where the bathroom is?" He took the pool stick out of her hand, as she walked down the hall with a soft 'yes'. Turning, he placed it up against the inside door jam and locked the door before going to the couch to sit down. God, he hoped he didn't get her sick; if he did, he'd take care of her, because it was his damn fault. Turning his head, he smiled as she came out of the bathroom, walked over to him and sat beside him on the couch.

"Mac, I don't think I can drive. I think I had too much to drink."

"Do you feel sick?"

"No, but I'm definitely buzzing big time and feeling happy."

Mac chuckled as the silliest grin come over her face. "Happy, huh?" He smiled as he leaned toward her, placing his lips against hers.

Sydney kissed him back, loving the feel of his lips against hers. She gasped when his teeth caught her bottom lip, his tongue running along the soft flesh. The heat within grew, the tingles numbing her brain. She moaned when his tongue darted into her mouth, tangling with hers. Sydney tightened her arms around his neck as his fingers slid into her hair near the back of her neck, traveling up to the back of her skull and releasing tons of electrifying tickles streaming through her body. Her chest rose, hard nipples grazed her bra as his mouth and hands worshipped her.

Breathing heavily, Mac moved his mouth off hers. Trailing kisses, he nipped her softly with his teeth along her jaw and down her neck. "Sydney, have you ever done anything you weren't supposed to?" he asked as he focused in on her neck.

"Once," she whispered into his ear, bending her head back so he could go to the other side of her neck.

"What?" He nipped the tendons on her upper shoulder, loving the way her sweet little body trembled against him.

"I, um…stole a pack of gum," she said in a breathless whisper.

Mac lifted his head, shocked. "You stole a pack of gum?"

"Yeah, when I was fourteen. But I felt so guilty, I went back and paid for it the next day."

Mac all but laughed, and then realized the buzz would be wearing off soon, and lowered his mouth to her neck, again working up to her ear. "That's it? You've never helped someone take anything?"

"No, that would be wrong." She sighed as his mouth covered hers again.

"Yeah, honey, that would be wrong." He lowered his mouth to hers again, his tongue sliding past her warm lips and into her hot sweet mouth, to find hers in heated meeting that had him groaning. "Is everything good with your family issue?"

"Which one?"

"The one you were distracted over when we first met."

Sydney tilted her head, his mouth on her neck and sighed. "That will never be all right."

"Why?"

"It's my sister, Lori." She groaned when he nipped the muscle between her shoulder and neck. "She's into drugs. When I don't give her cash, she gets nasty."

"She hasn't hurt you, has she?"

"No. Well, not physically. Oh gosh, Mac." Sydney grabbed his face between her hands and crushed her mouth to his. Sitting up a bit, she pushed back, causing him to lie on the cushions with her on top of him.

Mac wrapped his arms around her, spreading his legs and settled her against his hard cock. His tongue thrust into her mouth. "God, baby." Grinding his dick against her pussy, his hand moved to the back of her head, holding her as he attacked her mouth.

"Shit." Lifting his head when he heard a commotion down stairs, Mac sighed as he leaned away. "Stay here, I'll be right back." He rose up, heading for the door.

Sydney groaned as he shut it behind him, bringing her thighs together to ease the ache between them and could hear yelling making its way up the stairs. Laying her head back, she closed her eyes and felt the come down of the buzz.

"Honey, are you all right?" Mac asked, as her eyes fluttered open.

"I don't think I can drive."

"It's all right, you can stay here. Drink this for me." He held up a glass to her lips.

Sydney lifted her hand to bat him away. "No, I don't want any more to drink."

"It's water, I promise. It will help with the hangover in the morning." He put the glass to her lips so she could take a few sips.

"It's just coming off the buzz."

"I know honey, but it will still help so you don't get dehydrated and feel sick. Drink it slowly." Mac sat up with her for an hour, as he made sure she drank two full glasses of water. She was funny and blabbed about everything from her family to her work in between kisses, giving him a bit more insight into the world of Sydney Ripley and the answers he needed, until the buzz wore off.

"How are you feeling?"

"All right, but I have to go to the bathroom."

Mac smiled as he helped her up before walking behind her to the door. When she was done he handed her a pair of sweat pants. "Think you can get into them all right?"

"Yes, thank you," she said as she shut the door again. Pulling off her pants, she folded them before removing her bra from underneath her shirt, laying it into the folds of the pants. Why the hell had she drunk so much? She never did that, and now she looked like a total moron in front of him. When she walked out of the bathroom, she noticed that his bedroom light was on and stopped to watch as he pulled the sheets of his bed down, noticing that he had changed into sweats too and that was all he had on. Wow, what a body he had. He must have sensed she was staring at him, because he looked up with a smile.

"All yours," Mac said as he walked toward her. He led her to the bed and sat her on it, taking her socks off before having her lie back on to the pillows.

"Mac, where are you sleeping?" She grabbed ahold of his hand.

"On the couch." He kissed her gently.

"You can sleep on the other side. I mean, your bed is huge."

"Will you be comfortable with that?"

"Yes, as long as you promise to be good," she smiled.

"Honey, I'm never good, but I promise to behave." He climbed over her, staying on top of the covers as he brought her into his arms. "Good night," he whispered in her ear.

"Good night," she whispered back, feeling the brush of his lips on her temple. Closing her eyes, Sydney smiled as she drifted off into sleep.

Zack

~~*~~

Sydney cuddled into the warmth resting against her and peeped her eyes open, her lips turning up into a soft smile as she saw the man sleeping under her. Sometime during the night, she had rolled over to lay half on top of Mac, using his shoulder for a pillow. He looked so relaxed as he slept. Lifting her hand, Sydney drew a finger down his mustache, smiling when his mouth twitched and did it again. Her nose drew up into a crinkle when his lips moved from side to side. Lifting her finger, she waited until he was calm and then did it again, giggling when he mumbled something as he brought a hand up to rub his mouth. Damn, she was being so evil, but it was a fun evil. She waited until he flung his arm over his head before running her finger lightly over his bottom lip, gasping in surprise when his mouth opened, and his teeth caught her finger.

His green eyes twinkled with mischief. She smiled, gasping when he ran his tongue over her fingertip, sending thousands of tiny electric currents running through her and before she knew what was happening, he had her on her back. "I can torture just as well." Zack's voice low and husky. He lowered his mouth to hers.

Sydney wrapped her arms around his neck, he deepened the kiss.

Her groan sent his cock hard and aching. He heard the ring of his cell phone, her gaze heavy, half-lidded with desire as her lips parted, waiting for his kiss to continue. "Saved by the bell my lovely," he said with a smile as he rolled off her to grab the phone out of his jacket pocket. "Mac," he said as he sat down on the edge of the bed. "Why, what time is it?" he asked, looking at the clock. 8:05.

"Sorry-because I have company-no you cannot-try it and I'll kick your ass...I'll see you tomorrow--little shit, yeah bye," he finished as he hit the end button and then turned back to look at Sydney. "Brothers." He smiled as he lay back down on the bed.

"Were you supposed to meet him this morning?" Sydney asked.

"Yeah, an hour ago for breakfast."

"I'm sorry." She started getting up off the bed, only to have him grab her arm and bring her to lie on top of him, fitting her between his muscular thighs. Her stomach rubbed against his arousal.

"Don't be. We usually meet on Sundays for breakfast anyways."

Sydney looked down at him and then glanced at the clock. "Damn, I have to go," she said as she scooted off him.

"What do you mean you have to go?" He sat up, as she ran to the bathroom.

"Can I use your brush?" she called out through the door.

"Sure," he replied as he rose up off the bed, heading for the kitchen to start the coffee. Mac watched as she walked into the living room. "Your glasses are on the coffee table."

"Thank you." She grabbed a hair scrunch out of her purse, tying her hair back with it before picking up her glasses to put them on. When she looked up, Sydney found him staring at her.

"Coffee?" He held up a mug.

Sydney looked at the clock on the wall. 8:15. "Yeah, I have time for a cup." She walked up to the breakfast bar as he poured the steaming black liquid into a cup.

After setting it on the counter he opened the fridge, grabbed the milk and sugar, and placed them in front of her.

Sydney doctored up her coffee, sighing at the first sip.

"So, where are you off to so early on a Saturday morning?" Zack's gaze on her lips as they settled on the cup's rim and imagined them settling around his cock.

Sydney looked up at him. "You're going to laugh." she said, before taking another sip.

"Why would I laugh?" he asked, his eyes lifting to hers with a frown as she shrugged a shoulder.

"Every Saturday morning from nine to eleven I donate my time at the library, reading to the kids."

Mac leaned on the counter. "Why would I laugh at that?"

"Because I don't have a life." She chuckled.

"Honey, reading to kids is great. Not a lot of people take the time to, even though it's important." He leaned forward to place a soft kiss on her lips.

Sydney smiled at him when he backed away. "Lori calls me a goody-goody."

"Lori? Your sister?" he asked, as the smile disappeared from her face.

"Yes."

The hurt in her eyes yanked at his heart. "Don't listen to her. She's jealous because you're doing things she knows she should be doing," he said and kissed her again. "But we should get you going. I wouldn't want a bunch of kids mad at me for keeping their favorite reading teacher from them. Let me grab a shirt and I'll walk you down." He kissed her again before walking to the bedroom.

When he came out she was waiting for him by the door. "Can't wait to escape, huh?" he asked with a smile as he opened the door for her.

"I just don't want to be late. I'm never late and it will take me a half hour to get there."

"It's all right, honey. You won't be late," he said as they walked down the stairs.

~~*~~

Sydney was in a panic. "Oh my God, who would do this? Mac, who would do this?" she asked as she looked at her car. All four tires had been slashed.

"I don't know," he said, with a grim look on his face.

"How am I going to get to the library? My God, why would someone do this? What am I going to do?"

"It's all right, honey, I'll get you there."

"How?"

"I'll give you a ride."

"You'd do that?"

"Of course, I'd do that. Let's go." He grabbed her hand in his and led her around back to his bike. Mac stopped in front of the library, and helped her off the bike. "I'll be back at eleven to get you. Don't worry. I'll have your car fixed and ready to go."

Sydney smiled as she leaned down, brushing her lips across his. "Thank you," she said before turning and running up the steps of the library.

Mac waited until she was in the door before he took off, heading back to the Mer-Fay.

His brain turned at who in the hell had slashed her tires. At the next red light, he pulled his cell phone out of his pocket and called Walt, letting him know what happened and to keep his eyes open.

CHAPTER 5

MAC SMILED AS HE watched Sydney reading to the kids. They were so caught up in the story that not a one of them talked or fidgeted while she brought the story to life.

"Zackary Mac Cloud, what are you doing here?"

Mac winced as he turned to see his aunt standing behind him. "Hi, Aunt Ellie," he said as he leaned down to kiss her cheek. "Listen, I need you to do me a favor." His aunt raised an eyebrow. "You can't let Sydney hear you call me by my name."

"And why not?" she asked.

"You have to call me Mac, just Mac, nothing more."

"Just what is going on?"

Mac noticed Sydney was finishing up the story. "It's business," he said as he turned back to look at her.

"All right."

"Good. Pass it around the family, too."

"Can she know I'm your aunt?"

"Yeah, just no more than that."

"Mac, do you know Mrs. Hunt?" Sydney asked as she came up to stand beside them.

Mac turned around and smiled. "As a matter of fact, I do. She's my aunt."

"Your aunt?"

"That's right, and I fixed the problem with your car."

"Mac, tell me you didn't put her on the back of that monster," Ellie said.

"My Harley is not a monster, Aunt Ellie."

Ellie snorted. "Depends on who you ask. If you two will excuse me, I have work to do."

~~*~~

Sydney got off his bike after he parked it alongside her car. "Mac, those look like brand new tires," she said as she walked up to her car.

"They are; the others were too damaged and couldn't be fixed."

"But you didn't have to get new ones. They must have cost a good penny," she said, turning to look at him.

"That's what I pay insurance for."

"But won't that bring your premium up?" She watched as he shrugged his shoulder again. "Why didn't you just go to the junkyard and pick out some decent ones?"

"Because I'd rather you have good tires and not so-so ones you could get a flat with."

"I know how to change a flat."

Mac smiled. "I'm sure you do, honey, but that's not the point. Come on, let's go get something to drink," he said as he laid his hand at the small of her back, leading her around the building and up a flight of stairs. "Water or cola?" he asked as they stepped inside of his apartment.

"Water, please." She followed him and sat at one of the stools to the breakfast bar, her gaze following as he leaned in to the fridge. She couldn't help it. Her gaze went right to his butt; when he straightened up, she lowered her gaze to the counter as the heat on her cheeks enflamed.

Mac grinned as he turned around and saw her studying the counter. "It's not like I haven't checked out your butt."

Her gaze swung up. "You have not," she blurted out as he lifted an eyebrow. "W-when?"

"Every chance I get." His mouth turned up into a devilish grin.

"W-why?"

Mac's eyebrow went up. "What do you mean, why?"

"Do you have to answer a question with a question?"

"Yes."

"You know what? I think I should get going," she said as she jumped off the stool and headed for the door. "Thanks for letting me stay last night and for the ride this morning and for the tires and- bye." She rushed out and shut the door behind her.

Mac stayed where he was and waited; less than two minutes later there was a soft knock on the door. "It's open," he called out as it opened slowly.

Sydney winced as she stepped into his apartment again.

"Forget something?" He held her purse up and smiled.

"Yes, thank you." She went to take it.

Mac lifted it out of her reach, causing her to look at him. "Not until you answer my question."

"Y-you can't do that."

"Yes, I can," he said as he walked around the breakfast bar to stand in front of her.

"Th-that's- that's you're holding my purse hostage?"

"Am I?" He lifted it up out of her reach when she went for it again.

"I'm not answering you, so you might as well just give it back." She jumped for it and missed when he stepped back.

"You want your purse back?" he asked.

"Yes, please." Sydney frowned as he opened it. "What are you doing?"

Mac smiled when he spotted what he was looking for and took her keys out, putting them in his pocket as he handed her purse to her. "Your purse."

Sydney took her purse with one hand as she held the other one out, palm up. "My keys, please."

Mac patted his front pocket. "Right here, honey. Come and get them."

"Mac, I'm not sticking my hand in your pocket."

"Too bad, could be fun." His smile grew. "I guess you're just going to have to stay here until you answer my question."

Sydney kept a tight lip.

"It's your choice, honey."

"That's no damn choice at all and stupid, too," Sydney grumbled, eyes narrowing.

Mac kept her gaze as someone knocked at the door. "Come in."

"Mac, the whiskey guy's here. Hey doll," Walt said as he walked in.

"Hi, Walt." She didn't take her eyes off Mac.

"Well, it looks like we have a stand-off here." Walt said.

Mac leaned down, pressing a fast-hard kiss on her lips before heading for the door.

"Mac, give me my keys." Sydney turned.

Mac stopped with his hand on the door. "Answer my question." He stated.

"This is kidnapping," she said through clenched teeth.

"No, it's not. You can leave here any time you want. Just without the use of your car."

"Then it's car-napping," she said.

Mac hooted with laughter. "You better come up with something better than that. You know where the bedroom is, honey," he said as he shut the door.

Sydney stomped around the apartment for a while before stopping and heading for the door. Opening it, she looked both ways before heading for the back door and down the set of stairs. Rounding the corner, she noticed several people had already started to arrive. She went for her car, put her code in on the numeric keypad, opening her door. She popped the hatch to the trunk and walked around to the back. Reaching in, she pulled her tool box out and grabbed a screwdriver, black electrical tape and a utility knife. With that in hand, she headed back and lay down sideways on her seat as she unscrewed the screws holding the piece of plastic that was covering her steering column. After she took the covering off, she looked around at the wires, picking out the ones that she needed. She put the screwdriver on the passenger seat and picked up the utility knife, cutting both wires in half and then stripped some of the protective coating off each end before setting the knife aside.

"Oh, pray that I haven't lost my touch. Of course, this would have been a lot easier if I'd just put a spare in the glove box," she mumbled as she picked up two ends of the two different wires and twisted them together, then picked up the other two and touched them together, smiling when the engine started. "Oh yeah, tell me I can't have my keys. Just who does he think he is?" She grumbled, unaware she was being watched and heard. Sydney touched the gas with her elbow to give it a slight rev, and then twisted both wires together. "Go Sydney, go Sydney," she chuckled as she finished the last twist. She reached up to the seat, feeling around for the electrical tape. When she couldn't feel it, she looked up, meeting green eyes.

"Just what in the hell do you think you're doing?" Mac asked as he stood over her in the doorway.

Sydney jumped, knocking her head on the steering wheel. "Son of a bitch!" she yelled, slapping a hand to her forehead.

Mac reached in, turned off the music, and then backed up while she scrambled out from her car.

Sydney looked around at the crowd of male faces. "Giving that kid a lesson on, on how to steal my car the right way," she blustered, without looking at him.

"What kid?" Mac asked, trying to keep the smile at bay as he crossed his arms in front of him.

"That little kid. Didn't you see him? Short, real short, and black hair." Sydney blabbered as she scooted out of his way. "Hey kid, where'd you go?" she called out as she made her way to Walt. "Help me," she whispered.

"What?" Walt yelled. "Help you? Now why would I do that, doll?" He chuckled and had the other bystanders laughing.

When she saw Mac walking toward her, she scooted behind Walt. "Because he's bigger than me," she yelped.

"Now Sydney, why would a kid want to steal this hunk of junk?" Mac asked.

Poking her head out to the side of Walt's shoulder she said. "Hey, my car is not a hunk of junk, she's just an old lady." Stepping out beside Walt, she continued, "Besides, I wouldn't have had to hotwire her if you just gave me my keys."

"Which brings up the question, where did you learn how to hotwire a car?" Mac asked with a raised eyebrow.

"I-I used to repo cars."

"You used to repo cars?"

"Yeah, I had to pay for college somehow," she replied as she started walking toward him. "My keys, please." She held out her hand.

"What do you need them for? You started your car." He starting to reach into his pocket and then stopped. "That's right; you need your house key, unless you know how to break into houses, too." She looked at everything but him. "Sydney, you know how to break into houses?"

"I, um-learned how to pick locks."

"Well, Jesus, honey, what don't you know how to do?"

"A lot, okay? I told you I didn't have a life, so I taught myself how to do things. Why do you think your aunt knows me? Because I'm always at the library. That's why I was able to read to the kids."

"What do you read to them, Crimes 101?" Greeley asked.

Sydney turned around. "Shutup, Greeley." She started walking for her car. When she got to it, she kneeled in, untwisting the wires until the car shut off, and started twisting the right ones back together. Then she grabbed the electrical tape and wrapped both exposed areas, and proceeded to screw the covering back into place.

Gathering her tools, she put them back in her toolbox and shut the trunk. Shutting her door on the way by, she walked back the way she had come down.

When Mac came up to the apartment, she sat on the couch watching TV. Walking over to it, he shut it off and turned to face her. "Just because you won't answer a question?"

"It's not the question *per se*, just everything that comes

with the question," she sighed, hugging the pillow. Her heart rammed against her chest with the anxiety that always came when she had to think about her family, especially Lori. "All my life, I've been told how ugly I am, that I would never amount to anything. I knew I could change the 'amount to anything' part, but not the ugly part."

"My God, honey. You're not ugly," Mac said, as he sat in front of her on the coffee table.

"I know that, but I still question myself about it; my self-confidence lowers, especially when someone like you pays attention to me," she whispered, wondering why in the hell she was telling these things to him. Now he'd think she was clingy, someone who did anything to keep the attention of whomever was showing it to her. She knew men hated women with no self-confidence, or at least that's what she'd heard, and what does she do? She tells the most gorgeous, hottest, stud-muffin of a guy to ever pay attention to her that she has almost none.

Mac frowned. "What do you mean, 'someone like me'?"

"You're gorgeous."

"Honey, men are not gorgeous; we're handsome. Well, unless you're a drag queen."

Sydney glanced up at him and saw his smile. "The 'why' is because I know there are prettier women that have nicer butts, and it's hard to believe that-that you look at mine."

Mac leaned forward, placing a soft kiss on her lips. "Honey, that's not the only part I've checked out. You are a beautiful, sexy woman."

"Sexy?" she spat, making a face at him.

"Yes. Why do you think I always have my hand on your thigh when you ride with me? Especially when you have a skirt on." He smiled and wiggled his eyebrows at her. "It turns me on."

Sydney looked up at him, the heat going to her face. "I turn you on?"

"Yes, you do," he said, as he leaned in for another kiss. "And if you don't believe me, I'll show you." He brought her hand up to sit on top of his erection, watching as her eyes went wide.

"Whoa, crap. Mac?" she asked, as she moved her gaze from their hands to his eyes, her fingers moving along the hot thickness straining against his jeans. She felt the heat unfurl within her as the want and the lust to be with this man became abundantly clear.

"Yes," he replied as he moved her hand away. "Maybe it's not such a hot idea if you stay tonight," he said, as confusion skittered across her face. "If you did, I'd want you."

Sydney was confused. He'd kissed her, put her hand over his hard cock, and now he was pushing her away. Clearing her throat to give her brain a second to stop being mushy, she had to agree with him. "I suppose that's a good idea, seeing as how we haven't known each other that long."

"I know. That's why I'm sending you home," he said as he stood up, bringing her with him. "To remove the temptation." He smiled as he removed her keys from his pocket, handing them over to her. "I like you, Sydney, and I don't want to spoil it by jumping in the sack too soon," he said and then took her hand, walking her out of his apartment and down to her car.

"I'll see you later." Pressing his lips to hers, he held onto her for a moment longer as she responded and with a groan, he backed off. "All right, lady, off with you." Mac smiled as she got in her car, pulled out and drove down the road. Taking his phone from his pocket, he dialed and waited. "It's Mac."

"How'd it go?"

"She just left."

"Why?"

"Well someone forgot to tell me she could hotwire her car."

"What?!"

"That's right."

"Then you should have found another way."

Mac frowned. "And how the hell was I supposed to keep her here after that?"

"Who the fuck cares? Use your charms; we need the information. Screw her for all I care."

"You know, you make it sound so easy. Just screw her, huh? Well, trust me, she would if I encouraged it."

"Meaning?"

"She's had sex once if she's been lucky."

"Bullshit."

"No bullshit and I learned a lot last night."

"Enough for what we need?"

"Almost, there's still a few things I need to check."

"Fine, but we're running out of time."

"I know the fucking time table."

"Fine, bye."

"Yeah, bye." Mac hit the end button and put the phone back in his pocket, as he sensed a person behind him. "You know this is harassment, officer," he said without turning around.

CHAPTER 6

"WHY ARE YOU DOING this to her?" John asked as he stood behind Mac.

Mac turned around. "You know why, and you'll keep your mouth shut."

"Don't you hurt her; don't lead her on thinking you like her."

"I'll do what I have to, and you'll stay out of my way." Mac stepped up toe to toe, his face inches from John's. "You know what will happen if you interfere. Do you hear me?"

"Yes."

"Excellent, now be a good little copper and get lost." Mac walked by him, back to the bar.

~~*~~

Sydney left work a week later smiling; Mac had been waiting for her several times when she had gotten off work and they had eaten, talked and kissed. Walking over to the bench, she sat down to wait; he was supposed to be here to pick her up for dinner. The day had its down points, especially with Lori showing up again. This time Lori started in on her the minute she'd walked through the door. Tamara had to come out of her office and threaten

Lori with calling security if she couldn't keep her mouth decent. At that point, Lori flipped them both off and left.

Looking down at her watch, Sydney frowned. She'd been sitting there waiting for over an hour and it was already dark. "It's all right, something must have happened," she mumbled, as she rose up off the bench and started walking home, trying to keep her spirits high and her eyes open. She was halfway home when she heard a bike coming and stopped, turning as it came up to the curb next to her.

"I'm sorry," Mac said as he stopped the bike. "I had some moron walk in at the last minute with business."

"I- I thought you forgot?"

"No honey, I didn't forget. I'm hungry, how about you?" he asked, as he held his hand out.

Sydney glanced down at the hand offered and waited a moment before taking it. "I'm starving." A smile appeared on his face as she put her hand in his, sitting behind him on the bike.

"For a minute there I thought you were going to tell me to take a hike." He placed his hand on her bare thigh.

"For a minute there, I was."

"Well then, I guess I'm lucky you're starving."

Sydney met his gaze. "I guess you are." Leaning forward, she pressed her lips against his.

"I think I'd like Chinese food tonight."

"Sure honey, whatever you want."

~~*~~

Mac parked the bike in front of the Green Dragon and helped her off his bike. "You wanted real Chinese, right?"

"Yes, thank you." Sydney walked up to the door and

entered; Mac followed. She knew he was watching her as she settled the napkin over her lap.

"You're mad at me?"

"If I was mad at you, I wouldn't be talking to you and I wouldn't have kissed you."

Mac smiled. "But you're still upset or else you would've let me open the door for you."

"Let me guess, you're a psychologist in your spare time?" She snorted. "Of course, I'm still slightly upset; I don't like walking in the dark."

Mac reached over, taking her hand in his. "I'm sorry. It won't happen again." He lifted her hand, his lips placing feather-light kisses over her knuckles.

Sydney smiled at him. "See that it doesn't."

Mac's eyebrow lifted as he lowered their hands. "Since when did you get sarcastic and bossy? And here I thought you were some little mouse."

Sydney eased her hand out of his. "I am not a little mouse. Just because I don't stand up for myself all the time doesn't mean I can't." She lowered her gaze to the tablecloth.

"Damn it, I did it again. Boy, I'm batting one hundred tonight, huh?"

"Everyone thinks because I keep my mouth shut, that I'm easy to walk over. You know what, I am. I don't like confrontations and I back off even though I end up getting hurt in the process. So if you want to walk all over me, I think you better take me home now."

"Sydney, I don't want to hurt you." Leaning back when the waitress brought them their meal. Mac met her gaze "Do you want to eat, or do you want me to take you home?"

"I believe I offered you the choice." Sydney lowered her eyes, breath held as she waited.

"Then I suggest we eat before it gets cold." He held out a pair of chopsticks.

Sydney took the chopsticks. She hoped like hell she wasn't making a mistake. Even though she really liked him, she hadn't had the greatest track record when it came to boyfriends. By the time they finished eating, he had her laughing.

~~*~~

After parking the bike next to her car, Mac helped her off, both turning when they heard another car pull up.

"Hey, Sydney," came a female's voice.

Sydney smiled when she realized who it was. "Hi, Lisa. Lisa, Kevin, this is my friend Mac. Mac, these are my new neighbors."

Mac shook hands with Kevin. "Nice to meet you."

"You, too," Kevin said. "That your Harley?"

"Yeah."

"Nice ride."

"All right, you two," Lisa said, grabbing Kevin by the arm, pushing him away. "If I don't end this now, we girls will be in trouble." She laughed as she shoved him into their apartment and shut the door.

Sydney turned to look at Mac with a smile on her face. "They're newlyweds." She opened her door. Mac followed her inside, shutting it behind him.

"Friend? I thought I was a little more than that."

"You are. I mean, what are you doing?" she asked, as he dragged her into his embrace.

"Finishing what you started on my bike," he answered as his mouth swooped down to cover hers. His arms coming around her, he pulled her closer to him, and she gasped when she felt his erection rubbing against her thigh. Mac deepened the kiss as he dipped his tongue into her mouth, his hands finding her bottom, crushing her against his rigid cock as he squeezed the two round cheeks.

Sydney moaned, her arms going around his neck, the heat and lust pooling between her legs. She gasped as he backed her up to the door, lifting her.

Sydney knew what he wanted and tried to wrap her legs around him, but her skirt stopped her.

Both reached hands down to thrust the material up, her body trembling as his nails raked up her bare flesh. When she was free, he grabbed both of her thighs, lifting her up and settling himself between her legs. Sydney groaned, delving her fingers into his hair, twisting them in his thick curls as he attacked her mouth.

Mac grabbed her bottom, grinding her against his hardness as he squeezed. When she broke her mouth away gasping for air, he moved his down the side of her neck, nipping her before following with his tongue. "Are you protected?" he mumbled against her neck.

"N-no."

"Any condoms?"

"No," she whispered as she tried to breathe, her breasts hitting his chest with each indrawn breath.

Mac stopped, laying his forehead against her shoulder. "Shit."

"I-I don't even know if you're clean; we haven't talked about that."

"I'm clean, honey; I'm clean." He tried to get himself back under control.

"Me too," she answered as she leaned her head back

against the door. "I thought men were supposed to carry condoms in their wallets."

Mac chuckled. "Supposed to, yes. Do I, no." He placed a soft kiss against her lips when his phone rang. He took the cell out as he lifted his head. "Mac...yeah, I'll be right there." His eyes met hers as he hit the end button. "There's a problem at the Fay; I have to go." He backed away and helped her stand. They both brought their hands up at the same time to bring her skirt back down. Sydney chuckled nervously when she beat him to it. Mac put a finger under her chin, bringing her gaze up to his. "Are you all right?"

"Yes- I just- you don't think it's too, early do you? I mean, we've only known each other for about two weeks, I..."

Mac's kisses cut her off. "Does it feel right?" he asked as he backed up.

"It feels great, but I don't want to rush things."

"Then we won't, but it's been a hell of a time keeping my hands off you," he said and met her gaze. "Sydney, I've wanted you since the night you slept over." Leaning over, for a split second his lips touched hers. "I'll see you later. Lock it behind me." He opened the door, turning back for a quick kiss before stepping out on to her doorstep, and turned his head to the left, waiting until he heard Sydney slide the dead bolt.

"Kevin." He eyed the other man. He'd heard Kevin come out of his apartment after they'd entered Sydney's; that's why he put her up against the door. If the little bastard wanted to eavesdrop, he'd give him something to hear.

"Mac," Kevin said as he stood there with crossed arms.

Mac gave him a ghost of a smile before he got onto his bike and took off.

When Mac stopped at a red light, he took his cell phone out of his pocket, dialed and waited. "It's Mac. Since when do they send their own people in?"

"I don't know what you're talking about."

"Do you think I'm that stupid? Get them the fuck out of there or the deal is off."

"We can't just pull them out, it would look suspicious."

"Then you tell them to stay the fuck out of my way, until I get what I need." A muscle twitched along Mac's jaw as he hit the end button, not waiting for a response. Sliding the phone back into his pocket, he revved the engine and bolted when the light turned green. Parking his bike, Mac hopped off, striding into the Mer-Fay. Seeing who was waiting for him, he walked over to the end of the bar. "I got a call you have something for me." He growled as the bleach blonde turned from her conversation with one of his patrons, smiling.

"Well, yes I do," Lori said, as he motioned for her to go to the alcove.

Mac rolled his eyes at her swaying hips in the tight miniskirt, and realized that it did nothing for him. "What's up?" he asked as he sat down.

"First of all, I want the full two hundred this time or I go somewhere else." She picked up what little material there was of her tight shirt and removed a manila folder, putting it on the table in front of him before sitting down.

"First of all, I'm pretty pissed for being dragged away from something important, so don't even think to issue me ultimatums," Mac snapped as he sat up out of his slouch and opened the folder, flipping through several of the pages before shutting it. "Where'd you get this?"

"Same place as before." She smiled.

"You are either a very good klepto or very stupid. Don't you think they're going to start wondering where this information is going?"

"Who cares? It's not like they don't have backups. They'll most likely blame it on a secretarial error or something. What are you in such a bad mood for? I'm giving you good info, so hand over the money."

"That's bullshit, blondie, because you yanked me away from something pleasurable." He reached into his wallet, his fingers brushing up against the condom, wishing like hell he could have used it instead of lying to Sydney. He grabbed out two one hundred dollar bills and put them on the table.

"Well sexy, I can give you the pleasure part." Lori grabbed up the money, shoving it into her bra.

"And I told you, I like my ladies clean," he said, as he stood up with the folder in hand.

"Next time you have something for me, make sure you're here by five. I don't want you in this bar after five; do we understand one another?" He scrutinized her repulsive red pouting lips as she nodded. "Good, you can leave now," he stated as he walked away, meeting Walt's eye as he headed toward the stairs.

When Mac was in his apartment, he grabbed his cell phone. "It's Mac. Our informant was just here."

"Did she drop it off?"

"Yeah, I have the information."

"Did she mention anything about being helped?"

"No."

"Put it in the keep."

"Right." Mac said, hitting the end button as he headed for the back stairway.

~~*~~

"Yes, Officer Monroe, may I help you?" Tamara asked, as she walked out of her office the next afternoon.

John turned from Sydney's desk. "Can you tell me where Syd is?"

"She's at lunch right now; can I take a message?"

"No, I'd like to talk to her, if you could just tell me where she is, please."

"No, I don't think so," Tamara stated as she turned back to her office.

"Excuse me?" John asked.

Tamara turned her head, looking at him over her shoulder. "Did I stutter or did your ears wiggle? I said no."

"Miss Wong…"

Turning slightly, her eyes narrowed, and he stopped talking. "Officer Monroe, do you have any idea how much you've upset her? How stressed she is? She just had a blow out with Lori yesterday; she doesn't need one today. What do you two do, schedule your times so you can hit her while she's down from the other? Good day officer," she finished as she continued on her way to her office.

CHAPTER 7

TWO DAYS LATER, JOHN walked back into the office. Sydney was sitting at her desk.

"You haven't been returning my calls; I need to talk with you," he said as he stopped in front of her desk.

"I have nothing to say to you," Sydney replied without looking up. Damn him, she'd been engrossed in the paperwork before her and hadn't heard him approaching, or else she would have run like hell and hid until he'd left.

"Sydney, you stay away from him," he hissed.

"Why?"

"I can't say."

"John, kiss my ass." She jumped when he pounded his fist against her desk, her wide eyes lifting to him, first in fright, then in anger. "What the hell is wrong with you? Why can't you just let me be happy?"

"Because he's going to do nothing but hurt you, Syd. Do you want that?"

"What I want is a chance, John, a chance to try and be happy. But every time I try, you scare them away."

"That's because I don't want to see you hurting again like in college, you're like my sister, Syd."

"I know, John, but you have to let me live my own life."

Sighing, John nodded his head, turned and left without saying another word.

Two minutes later the phone rang. Breathing deeply, Sydney forced a smile as she answered. "Assistant D.A. Wong's office, may I help you?"

"Sydney, what's wrong?"

"Mac?" She grabbed a tissue off her desk, bringing it up to her eyes.

"Yeah, honey. Have you been crying?"

"I-I'm fine."

"That's not what I asked."

Sydney closed her eyes to calm herself. "I'm fine."

"I was calling to see if you wanted to have dinner tonight."

"Yeah, I'd love to."

"I'll pick you up at five, then."

"Five it is."

"Great. See you then."

"Okay, bye."

"Bye."

~~*~~

Mac was there before five. He smiled as she walked down the steps, her hair swaying from side to side, his fingers tingling with the urge to rake them through her long silken locks. He studied her face and body language, finding no signs of the distress he'd heard earlier in her voice.

"Well, don't you look like a bad boy with that bandana around your head," Sydney teased as she walked up.

His lips tilted up with a devilish grin. "And you like it, don't ya'?" He held out his hand and helped her seat herself behind him.

Sydney looked up to his sunglass-covered eyes. "Yes." She leaned around to kiss him. "Where are you taking me for dinner?"

"Where do you want to go?" His hand settled on her thigh.

"How about the Fish Shack? I have a hankering for something fried."

"Sounds good to me; hold on, honey," he said, smiling when she wrapped her arms around him, her hands crossed and resting on his chest. Damn, she was making him horny. He looked over his shoulder before he pulled the bike away from the curb.

"Mac, why you look like a hoodlum when you bring pretty lady back? You suppose to look nice when taking her out," Lei said, as she walked up to their table and playfully smacked him upside the head.

"Come on, Lei, I had business." He ducked her hand the second time.

"You business get you in big trouble with lady; you look good when come here next time, eh."

"What do you want me in, a suit?"

"Not that drastic and get a haircut, shave, not a snot rag on your head."

Mac belted out a roaring laugh, as Sydney chuckled. "You sound just like my mom. My God, give me a break."

"Yes, I talk with Mom. She agrees; says you better dress nice for brother's wedding. I be there; you look nice, eh."

"I have no choice. I have to wear a monkey suit."

"Then no act like monkey. You bring pretty lady?" She looked over at Sydney.

"If you'd stop ragging on me I might have a chance to ask her."

Lei laughed. "I go now; you ask." She walked away.

Mac took his glasses off as he grinned at Sydney. "Well, what do you say?"

Sydney squirmed in her chair. "You don't have to ask just because she brought it up in front of me."

"I'm not asking because Lei brought it up. Do you think I'd let someone push me into something?"

"No," she answered with a soft smile.

"Good. That's why I asked you to dinner tonight, to see if you wanted to go. So, Sydney Ripley, would you like to be my date to my brother's wedding?"

"Yes."

"Great. It's this Saturday at one." He rose up out of his chair, gathering up their trash.

"That's in two days! Are you crazy? I don't have a dress to wear."

"Then go shopping; but remember, nothing too tight. We're taking the bike."

"Taking the bike to a wedding—you are nuts." She followed him to the trash can. "And I hate shopping."

Mac turned around. "You hate shopping? I thought women loved to spend money."

"Well, I don't. Can't we take my car?"

"I'd rather take the bike. It's not that far from your place. Hey, where are you going?" He asked, as she started walking the other way.

"To tell Lei you want to take the bike."

Mac grinned as he ran after her. Catching her, his arms wrapped around her, bringing her back up against his chest as he twirled around. "Oh, no, you don't; I've been ragged on enough for one day," he said as she laughed. "Oh, you're a minx." He pressed a smiling kiss on her lips as he lifted her feet off the ground and carried her over to his bike.

"Is that a gun in your pants, or are you just happy to see me?" Sydney asked as he carried her.

Mac looked up with a smile. "What do you think?" He wiggled his eyebrows at her, causing her to laugh again.

"Are you going to be able to drive with Mr. Happy?"

"You shouldn't say things like that."

The smile slid from her face. "You don't like it?" she asked warily.

"Oh, honey, I like it well enough, so well that if you don't stop I'm going to take you against that tree right now," he promised huskily, as he pushed her harder toward his erection.

"Oh." She blushed.

"You shouldn't do that either." He slid her down the length of him until her feet touched the ground.

"Do what?"

"Blush. It makes me horny."

Sydney laughed again. "What doesn't make you horny?"

"Nothing when you're around," he said, swooping down for a kiss before helping her on the bike.

Mac turned his head as a car came up alongside of them. Slowing the bike, he pulled over to the curb.

"Why are we stopping?" Sydney asked.

Shit, he didn't want to do this now, especially with Sydney on the back of his bike. Nothing like jumping feet first into the frying pan from the fire. "Listen. Don't talk, move, nothing, unless I tell you to. Go along with what I say and do not look any of them in the eye. Keep yours to the ground."

"What?"

"Just do it," Mac ordered harshly as he got off the bike and walked up to the car stopped in front of them. He heard the confusion in her voice, and hoped like hell she'd listen to him or else it could mean both their lives.

Several men exited the car. Sydney did what Mac said; she looked to the ground. She couldn't understand them, but Mac could because he was talking to them. After a few minutes they turned to English.

"Is she your woman?" She heard one of them ask and felt her heartbeat accelerate to a pounding beneath her ribs.

"Yes," Mac replied.

"You, woman. Come here," one of them ordered, but Sydney stayed where she was.

"She's trained, Chang, and won't unless I tell her to."

What the hell was that supposed to mean—trained, trained in what, she thought.

"Then tell her to."

"I don't mean to be disrespectful, but I'm on my way to a job after I drop her off."

"I need to meet with you, tonight."

"I'll be there."

Mac winced when Chang walked to his bike, reached out and caressed Sydney's breast. Thank God, she didn't move an inch.

"You sell her to me, Mac; she'd make a good mistress,"

Unclenching his jaw, he breathed deeply. "Now why would I do that when you have two wives and three mistresses, and I have one? Take pity on me, Chang; I train a woman right and you want me to sell her to you?"

"I told you to take young woman; they a lot more trainable than the older ones. When you tire of her, you call me," he said.

Sydney listened to their car drive away.

"They're gone. Christ, honey, are you all right?" Mac asked as he stepped toward her.

When Sydney looked up at him he almost stepped back. She was pissed. "Take me home, now!" Her voice was filled with anger and hurt.

Mac ran a hand over his face. "Sydney" he said.

Her lips tightened and her eyes focused on the handlebars. Mac got on the bike and pulled away from the curb, heading to the Mer-Fay instead of her house.

When he parked the bike on the side of the bar and got off he turned, waiting for her to do the same. After several moments he walked back over to her. "Let's go," he said softly.

"I told you to take me home," she said through clenched teeth, not bothering to look at him.

"I'm not taking you home until we talk," he replied, standing there for several more Minutes, waiting for her. God, he knew she was pissed; emotions for her aside, he had to handle it now, before she had time to think their so-called relationship through and salvage what he could until his time was up. "We either do this the easy way, which is you walking in, or we do this the hard way, which is me carrying you. Which do you want?" he asked, and ended up standing there for several more minutes.

Oh, she was pissed right now; all she wanted to do was go home and have a good cry. Rising up off the bike, she straightened her skirt and turned around, walking back out to the road. She didn't get five steps when Mac grabbed her by the arm, turning her around. She didn't get a chance to do anything, because the next thing she knew, she was being thrown over his shoulder, having the wind knocked out of her.

Mac lifted one hand to the hem of her skirt to make sure it didn't fly up as his palm hit the door, swinging it open hard.

"What the hell do you have there, Mac?" Greeley called out. "Holy shit, is that Sydney?"

"Sydney?" came a high-pitched female voice that made Sydney wince. "I should have known that ugly suit and fat ass anywhere."

Sydney tried to sit up on his shoulder. "Put me down now!" She hissed.

Mac glanced at her and did as she asked. When she stood on her feet she gave him a mean look before turning around to see her sister. Mac gave Lori a mean look of his own.

"You turned me down for her?" Lori whined, already half drunk.

"I told you, I like my ladies clean." Mac said, as she snorted.

"Is this why you told me not to come in after five? Because of her?" Lori swayed as she talked, her hand going out to catch herself. "Jesus Christ, Mac. You could have done better than my..."

"Lori!" Sydney yelled. "I'm not in the mood for your mouth right now."

Lori laughed. "You're a mousy little bitch," she slurred to Sydney, and then looked at Mac. "I can't believe you're fucking her. She's not good, trust me. The one guy..."

"Lori, shut your mouth!"

"Or you'll what? Cry like you did in college," she said, rubbing her fists over her eyes as she laughed. "Because I had to…"

"I'm warning you!" Sydney said as she took a step forward.

"…Pay the guy from the fraternity who won the bet and actually got in her pants," Lori said, laughing.

"Son of a bitch!" Sydney shouted as she came forward. Her hand fisted and up, she swung, punching Lori in the face. "I told you I wasn't in the mood," she said, as she hit her with her other fist. "I'm sick of you being mean to me!" Bringing her right hand up, she knocked Lori so hard in the nose that Lori went down. Sydney came to stand over her and lifted her up by her threadbare shirt. "You stay the hell away from me, Lori. Do you hear me? Do you hear me?" She panted as she watched her sister nod.

Letting go, Sydney let her sister fall to the floor. Straightening up, she brushed her hair back over her shoulder, stood there for several seconds, her chest heaving with deep breaths, before walking to the back and up the stairs. Her eyes focused on that one place; the bar was dead silent and she was afraid to look anyone in the eye.

Mac looked at Walt. "Get her out of here and the rest of you keep your mouth shut," he said as he followed Sydney up the stairway. Ninety-five percent of the men in his bar were like him; the others, well, they knew to keep their mouths shut. Now he hoped like hell that Lori hadn't lost her only revenue into the D.A.'s office. Stupid, damn druggie.

Sydney staggered up the stairs, tears pooling in her eyes. She let out a cry when she looked down at her hand, as she grabbed the door knob and saw blood. Shoving the door open, she staggered into the bathroom, banging her shoulder against the doorjamb. Turning on the water, she ran her hands under it, letting the coldness take some of the pain away. Glancing up, she saw her image in the mirror. She had tears running down her face and her eyes were puffy. Her whole body trembled as she cupped water in her hands, splashing water onto her face. She was so damn exhausted from Lori and John, and now Mac with the incident tonight.

Mac walked in his open door, shutting it behind him before going toward the sound of running water. Silently he stood there and watched her shaking body. When she laid her head down on her arm, he stepped into the bathroom and shut off the water. Placing his arm under her knees, he lifted her into his arms, carrying her to the bedroom. Placing her on the bed he unbuttoned her jacket, sliding it off her as she sat there. He grabbed some sweats and a t-shirt out of his bureau and laid them on the bed before he walked over to kneel in front of her. "Can you change by yourself?" he asked softly.

Sydney nodded.

"All right, I'll be back in a bit." He rose up, pressing his lips to her forehead before walking to the door, shutting it as he passed through. Going downstairs, he went to the bar and had Walt pour him some brandy.

"She all right?" Walt asked, as he set the glass down on the bar.

"She will be; she's still shaking a bit."

"Want to tell me why she's pissed at you?"

Mac sighed as he raked his fingers through his hair. "Because after dinner, Chang pulled us over."

"Oh shit, she must have loved that."

"Yeah, especially when he offered to buy her."

Walt chuckled. "You're shitting?"

"Did she look like I'm shitting?"

"Does she know?"

"No, and if I can do some fancy footwork, she won't." Mac picked up the glass of brandy and walked back up the stairs. Once in the quietness of his apartment, he stopped in the bathroom for some antibiotic medicine and bandages before knocking on the bedroom door as he opened it. He saw her lying on the bed as he walked over to her, setting the bandages and medicine on the night table. "Here honey, drink this," he said, as he helped her sit up.

Sydney sipped it and then put the glass on the night table as he picked up the medicine, laying it on the bed as he lifted her hand and set it on his thigh.

It bothered him that she remained silent while he applied the medicine and bandages to both hands. Mac was setting the medicine on the night table when she spoke.

"Why did you let him touch me like that?" Sydney asked softly.

Mac turned. "Honey, I know this is going to be difficult to understand, and I'm asking you to bear with me. There wasn't much I could do unless we were married; he is a very important man."

"Then why didn't you tell him we were married, instead of letting me be humiliated?" she asked, as she lifted her eyes to him.

Mac lifted a finger, trailing it down the side of her jaw. "I think he would have noticed no wedding bands, don't you?"

"Are you doing illegal things with him?"

"No."

"Have you?"

"In the past we have had dealings."

"But you're not now?"

"No Sydney, I'm not. I promise you, I'm not," he whispered as he laid the side of his head against hers, the tremors still going through her as the adrenaline subsided. "Lie down, honey. You need to try to get some sleep," he said as he laid her down, bringing the covers up over her.

"Mac, I can't stay. I have work in the morning."

"So call in."

"I can't call in; I've never called in."

"And you've worked there how long?"

"Two years."

"Uh huh, I don't think they'll fire you for taking a day off. Now lie back down, let the adrenaline rush leave you, and go to sleep." He leaned down, placing a kiss on her lips.

Sydney backed away and met his gaze. "Mac. Don't ever let anyone humiliate me again."

"I won't, honey."

"You promise?"

"Yes, I promise."

"That's good, because I don't think you want to see me mad again."

"God, anything but that," he said with a smile, as he leaned down brushing his lips across hers. "I have some paperwork to finish downstairs; I'll be back in a little while. Get some sleep, okay?" He kissed her one more time before rising off the bed.

CHAPTER 8

SYDNEY MOANED AS SHE rolled over onto her back. Her eyes fluttered open to see Mac climbing into bed. "What time is it?" she asked groggily.

"After two." Mac rolled onto his stomach, holding himself up by his elbows as his head lowered, his lips caressed hers gently.

"I have to go; I have work in the morning."

"It's all taken care of."

"What is?" Sydney asked as she met his gaze.

"I went to your apartment earlier to get you some clothes and saw your boss's number on the fridge, so I gave her a call."

Sydney was surprised, to say the least. "You called Tam; what did you say?"

"I told her that Lori gave you a real hard time tonight, that you'd be staying with me, and I asked if she'd mind if you took a personal day tomorrow." He brushed a wayward strand of hair, off her forehead.

"And what did she say?"

"She said you should have taken one a few days ago and she'd see you on Monday," he said, before leaning down to place another soft kiss on her lips. "I gave her my cell number in case of some secretarial emergency, so you can sleep as late as you want in the morning. Okay?" He rolled over onto his back.

"Do you want some of the covers?" Sydney asked, as she rolled onto her side to face him. God, what Tam must be thinking.

Mac turned his head to look at her. "I don't think that would be a good idea, honey," he said, but wanted nothing more than to jump under the covers with her and rip his sweats off her.

"Night, Mac." Her eyes started to flutter.

"Night, honey."

~~*~~

Sydney awoke slowly as she rolled onto her back, stretching her hands above her head with a groan. She flopped them down on the pillow, opening her eyes to see Mac standing over her smiling.

"Well, Sleeping Beauty decides to wake up after all."

"What time is it?"

"Eleven." He sat on the bed.

"Eleven?"

Mac handed her a cup. "Coffee, two sugars, light."

Sydney took the mug he offered. "Yes, thank you," she replied, and then took a sip of the warm brew. "I can't believe I slept this late."

"It's your body's way of telling you it needs rest."

"I get enough sleep."

"What about stress?"

"Everyone has stress," Sydney said and took another sip.

"Then why did your boss say you should have taken a day off days ago; what's been going on, Sydney?"

Sydney ran a hand through her hair. "Between Lori and John badgering me."

"At work?" he asked with a frown.

"Yeah, as Tam puts it, they must schedule around each other. One will come in one day and then the other one comes in another."

"I can see John going to your work, because of him being an officer, but why would Lori go to the court house?"

"Because she wants me to give her money."

"Money, money for what?"

"Drugs, and every time I tell her no, she's just nastier to me; like the last time she came in, she didn't even bother asking for money; she started on me like she did last night. Tamara had to threaten to call security if she didn't leave."

"And what happened yesterday when I called?"

"That was John's turn. Does Lori usually come in here?" she asked as she met his gaze.

"No, although she has been in a few times trying to sell some stuff." Mac said, his gaze on her and her facial expressions.

Sydney frowned. "Sell stuff? Is she selling drugs or, or, oh God, tell me she's not prostituting." Her eyes widened at that horror.

Mac regarded the emotions in her eyes as well as her facial features; she was either not a very good poker player or she was a very good actress. He was steering toward the first option, but one never knew. "Not that I know of, honey," he said, as he leaned down to kiss her. "I put your things in the bathroom, so when you're ready, we can go find you a dress." He smiled as he rose up off the bed.

Sydney met him in the living room after she had showered

and dressed. "Are you sure you want to go shopping with me?"

"Sure, why not?" He grabbed his sunglasses off the coffee table.

"Because I'm not a shopper. I go in and if it looks like it fits then I get it."

A smile tugged his lips as she walked toward him. "Well then honey, I'm going to have to introduce you to a thing called the dressing room." He chuckled, his hand on her lower back as he escorted her out.

~~*~~

Mac took the bag from Sydney before helping her off the bike. "Do you want to stay and play pool for a while?" he asked as they walked up the back stairs of the building.

"Are you so eager to get your butt kicked?" She followed him up.

Mac looked at her as they reached the door. "I'm sorry; I thought I was the one who kicked your butt the last time?" He opened the door to his apartment.

"That's because I had too much to drink," she said, closing the door as she walked in.

"And that won't happen tonight."

"So sure of yourself, huh?" He took her new dress out of the bag and walked to the bedroom to hang it up.

"Yes. I am."

"Miss Cocky tonight," he said, as he walked out of the bedroom toward her, taking her into his embrace. "Thank you for lunch." He bent down to kiss her.

"It was my turn; you've been springing for everything," she said, before standing on her tiptoes to kiss him back. Wrapping her arms around his neck, she took over the kiss, sliding her tongue into the warmth of his mouth and moaned. She wanted to see how far he would go. So far she'd slept over twice and he hadn't tried anything more than kissing and heavy petting. The last time she'd felt his hard cock pressing against her was when he'd put her hand on him and then pulled back, except for the night when neither of them had any protection. She knew better this time because she'd seen some condoms in his shaving kit when she had asked to borrow a razor this morning. Sydney twined her fingers in his hair, following the bottom of his lip with her tongue.

Mac groaned as he brought her up against him, his hands traveled the length of her back to stop and cup her bottom with each hand, bringing her warmth up against his hard-on.

Sydney moaned at the length of him rubbing against her and dipped her tongue into his mouth, meeting his, where he took over with frenzy.

Mac could hear her heavy breathing, her heart beating rapidly against his chest as he took his mouth away and moved it down her neck.

Sydney moved her hands all over him, from his hair to his shoulders and biceps. When he hit a sensitive spot, she heard herself gasp with the pleasure spreading out to her limbs, her fingers tightening on his shoulders as she arched her body against his.

Mac lifted his head, planning on attacking her mouth again when he heard a knock at the door. Groaning, he laid his head in the crook of her neck. "Yeah?" he called out.

"It's Walt, you're needed downstairs."

Sydney heard the retreat of footsteps as she tried to get her breathing under control.

"I'm needed downstairs."

Sydney shivered as his hot breath hit the side of her neck. "Yeah."

Mac lifted his head, pressing his lips firmly on hers before heading toward the door.

Sydney stood there as he left, blowing a wayward strand of hair out of her face. She stomped to the bathroom in frustration. What in the hell could demand his presence downstairs? It was only four in the afternoon, for Pete's sake.

Walt turned as Mac came down stairs. "Are you all right, boy?"

"Yeah, you came just in the nick of time," Mac replied as he walked over to the bar.

"Maybe you shouldn't be spending so much time with her alone."

"No choice." He grabbed a soda.

"Then you better watch yourself before you get something you don't need- trouble."

"Trust me, I've been trying. I can't just stop or else she'd know something was up."

"Can't or won't?" Walt asked, looking at him with a smile.

Mac's hands came up to cover his face. "It's not that easy."

"I know boy, but remember the job," Walt said, as he slapped a hand on Mac's shoulder.

"Come on, straighten up; she'll be down here in a few," he said as he put some papers on the counter. "Problems with a distributor."

Sydney walked down the stairs with pool stick in hand. Spotting Mac sitting over at the bar she walked to him. "Hey you, ready for that pool game?"

"Sorry, honey, I can't; we're having a problem with one

of our distributors. There was supposed to be an order here today and they're telling us they can't make it."

"Are you running low?"

"Yeah, you know what, honey? I called you a cab to take you home. It should be here in about five minutes."

That was the last thing she'd expected. "Y-you called me a cab?" she asked in shock.

"Yeah, I won't have any free time to spend with you, and I don't have the time to take you home right now."

Sydney was flabbergasted. "Oh, ah, okay." She didn't know what to say; she didn't think he'd send her home just because of a distributor problem. "I- I guess I'll go get my things," she said softly as she turned around, heading back up the stairs.

She stuffed most of her purchases in her overnight bag and hefted it onto her shoulder when she heard a car horn beeping. Grabbing her dress, she walked out of the door and turned to the back stairway instead of going down through the bar. She was hurt, and didn't want to see him right now. A distributor problem wouldn't take all night to fix; she knew it was busy on Fridays, but he'd made time for her before. It wasn't like he had to babysit her; she could play pool or something. In truth, she was disappointed as well; she'd wanted to spend the night with him, sleep next to his strong muscular body again and hopefully do a little more than kiss. With a heavy sigh, she headed down the stairs and out the door.

After paying the cabbie, she took her keys out of her purse and grabbed her bags out of the cab.

Sydney put the key in the lock and opened the door, dropping everything in the doorway as she stood looking at her apartment in shock. "Oh my God," she said, as she stared at her living room. Turning, she saw the cabbie getting ready to take off. "Wait!" she yelled as she ran up to him as he stopped the car.

"You forget something?" he asked as she came around to the drivers' side.

"N-no, I-I n-need y-you t-to…"

"Easy lady, what's wrong?" He got out of the cab.

"M-my apartment." She pointed to her open door. "S-someone b-broke in."

~~*~~

Sydney was still shaking when John pulled up in his cruiser. "John."

"Syd, are you all right?" he asked as he knelt down. "God, Syd, you're shaking like a leaf," he said bringing her into a hug. "It's all right, Cuz. It's all right."

After awhile, one of the detectives came out to stand next to them. "Ma'am, do you think you can go through and see if anything was taken?"

Sydney looked up at John. "Will you come with me?"

"Yeah, let's go."

They spent an hour going through her apartment. "I-I just don't see anything missing; all my jewelry is there."

The detective nodded. "Does someone have a grudge against you?"

"Not that I know of. Why?"

"Because every picture we found of you has in one way or another been destroyed. We think it may be someone you angered."

"What about that guy you've been hanging out with?" John snorted.

"No, that's where I just came from, but last night, Lori and I got into it and I hit her, several times."

"Hit her?" John asked. His eyebrows lifted.

"Yeah, I kicked the crap out of her, gave her a bloody nose and knocked her down."

"Damn, what the hell did she say?"

"The same thing you keep pissing me off about. College and what happened."

"Has Lori ever been here?"

"No."

"Detective, can you run the prints up against Lori Ripley's? They're already on file."

"Yeah, not a problem. Ma'am, do you have some place to go tonight?"

"No."

"Syd, go to Mom's house; you know you can," John said.

"I know, but this is my home, and I need to start cleaning it anyways."

"Are you sure?"

"Yeah, I'll be all right."

"Okay, I'll just fix the back window before I leave."

"Thanks, John."

"Monroe, I'll let you know what I come up with," the detective said, as he walked out the door.

Sydney had her bedroom picked up and started on the living room when John came out of the back room. "It's all set, locked and secured."

"Thanks, John."

"No problem. Oh, by the way, while you were outside, your friend called," he snorted, as he started for the door.

"Mac called and you didn't tell me?"

"I figured you had enough to deal with."

"Who answered the phone?"

"Me. I'll talk to you tomorrow; don't forget to lock the door when I leave."

Sydney walked over, locking the door. She eyed the phone, knowing that Mac had called because she left the back way. Her anger for him was gone with the excitement of the break-in. Sighing, she walked over to the phone. "Might as well get one more stressful moment over with," she muttered as she dialed the Mer-Fay's number. "Hi, Walt. Is Mac there? It's Sydney," she said and waited while he yelled for Mac.

"Why'd you leave the back way without saying goodbye?" Mac asked as he picked up the phone.

Sydney could hear the anger in his voice. "You looked busy and I didn't want to bother you." She fidgeted with super gluing a vase back together.

"Come on, Sydney. That's bullshit and you know it."

"I-I'd- don't you swear at me."

"Sorry," he said, blowing out a breath. He raked his fingers through his hair as he stared at the back wall. He was frustrated, damn it. He'd heard the cab beeping for her and when she hadn't come down after five minutes, he'd gone up to check on her to find his apartment empty. He didn't need her pissed at him, he couldn't afford it and neither could the people he worked for, not until they were done with her. Listening as she breathed into the other end of the phone. "You pissed at me?" he finally asked.

"Not so much."

"Then why'd it take you four hours to call me back?"

"B-because there was something I had to take care of."

Mac listened to her stuttering and knew something was going on. "Sydney, what's wrong?"

"Nothing."

Mac narrowed his eyes when her breathing escalated. "Honey, what happened, why was John there?" He asked as Walt's head whipped around to look at him.

Sydney couldn't help it; she started crying.

Mac's heart pounded against his chest as he listened to her sobs. "Honey, what happened?"

"My, s-someone b-broke in and broke everything."

Mac jumped up from the bar and ran out the door.

Walt picked up the phone and heard her crying. "Doll, it's Walt. Mac's on his way." Walt stayed on the phone with her until Mac arrived.

~~*~~

Mac's stomach tightened as he sped down the street; Sydney was work, and he was getting too involved with her emotionally. His heart pounded. His boss would yank him if he found out and then there would be hell to pay. He couldn't keep doing both; he had to pick one: Sydney or the job. "Son of a bitch." Pushing away was what he should be doing, even as he raced like hell to get to her. Jumping off the bike, he ran up to her door. "Honey, it's Mac," he said, watching as she opened the door and hung up the phone. He closed and locked the door. Turning, he brought her into his arms. His gaze moved over the interior mess and he cringed. She had picked up and put most things back in their places, but broken items were laid about here and there, her couch pillows and chairs had been cut with stuffing popping out everywhere. Her drapes were torn to shreds still hanging on their poles, and her TV, DVD player and stereo were all smashed, stacked to the side in a pile. "Honey, does John know who might have done this?"

"Lori," she mumbled against his chest.

"Lori, your sister?"

"They took fingerprints and are running them against hers."

Mac walked her over to the couch and with one hand, flipped the couch cushions one by one before helping her sit down. "She wasn't here when you came in, was she?"

"No, she'd rather do it when she knows she won't be caught."

"Was the rest of the apartment torn up?"

"Yes."

"How'd she get in?"

"Through the back window, but it's okay, John fixed it."

Mac cupped the side of her face with his hand. "Are you okay?" he asked.

She nodded her head. "Yeah, just tired, I guess."

"How does your bedroom look?"

"All right. She didn't touch anything except for my work clothes."

"What'd she do?"

"Cut them up."

"All of them?"

"Yeah, I guess I need to go shopping before Monday, huh?" She lifted tear-glazed eyes to his.

"Ah honey," Mac wrapped his arms round her. "Come on, let's get you into bed." He stood, lifting her into his arms.

"Mac, I can walk."

Mac smiled as he looked at her. "Let me be chivalrous. I feel bad enough I sent you home in a cab when you should have been at the Fay with me." He walked down the small hallway, spotting her bedroom from the open door; turning them both sideways, he walked in setting her down on the bed. "Have you eaten yet?"

"No."

"All right, let me go see what you have."

"I'm not very hungry."

Mac leaned forward, kissing her lightly on the lips. "Change, and I'll see what I can find." He straightened up and walked out of the room.

Sydney scooted off the bed. Stepping over to the dresser, she pulled out a t-shirt and some pajama bottoms. After changing, she walked out to the kitchen and sat at her small round table, as Mac opened the microwave, taking out a steaming bowl.

"All I could find was chicken soup." He set the bowl and a spoon down in front of her.

Picking up the spoon, she blew on a spoonful of broth mixed with noodles before bringing it to her mouth, aware of him watching every move she made. After eating half of the bowl she pushed it away. "Can I ask why you sent me home?" She glanced up.

"I told you why."

"Because of a distributor problem?"

"Yeah."

Sydney took a deep breath, exhaling it slowly as the hurt and anger from before came back. "Please give me more credit than that. I'm not stupid."

"I never said you were."

"Then don't lie to me."

"Sydney," he said, as she held up a hand to silence him.

"Please don't. I think I've been a little too trusting. I could have pushed you more on the incident the other night with your buddy Chang, but I didn't. I could have done the same thing with Lori being in the bar and a few other things that I've taken your word for. I'm not blind nor am I slow, so don't treat me like an idiot, and while I'm on a rant here, I'd like to know why every time we start getting hot and heavy someone is always there interrupting and no matter what it is, you always go running. I'd like to know why you haven't even tried making a move on me. Every time we kiss, I've been the one to take it a little farther. Sure you've been sweet and gentlemanly; I've slept over at your place twice and you've barely tried to feel me up. Is it just me or is there something else going on?" she asked as she sat there, her gaze on him. No emotions whatsoever came over his features; he wouldn't even look up at her and that twisted her stomach. Was what he'd told her about Chang and everything else a lie?

"Sydney, you have been trusting and I appreciate that; there are things I can't discuss with you right now. I'm not doing anything illegal, I promise you. And as for always being interrupted--I'm sorry, I own a business and I'm the only one who can take care of certain things. I don't think you're an idiot, and you know how my body reacts when I hold you."

Sydney's head hung down until her chin rested on her breastbone, as she thought about his words. "Yeah, I know, I-I still feel you're hiding something from me, but I'm going to let it drop for the night because I'm tired, and I'd really like to go to bed now." She rose out of her chair, heading to the bathroom.

Raking his hand through his hair, he blew out a deep breath. God, he was going to blow this if he wasn't careful.

What the hell was it about Sydney Ripley that had him this close to chaos? Christ! Walt was already starting to judge his perception. What the hell was he going to do if Walt informed his superiors? When she walked out of the bathroom, Mac was there waiting for her. "Do you want me to sleep on the couch? I'm asking because you don't seem too sure of me at the moment."

"I'm not too sure of anything now. So, hop in the bed; it's big enough and you're at least a foot or two longer than the couch." She walked over to the bed, letting out an exhausted sigh as she lay down.

Mac walked over to the other side, sitting down on the edge, and started to take his boots off. "Do you want me to stay dressed, or can I sleep in my underwear?" When she didn't answer, he turned to look at her over his shoulder and found her asleep. Rolling onto the bed, he leaned over, pressing his lips to hers before rolling onto his back and closing his eyes.

Mac jumped out of bed, scanning the room. Something had woken him up. Looking over at Sydney, he saw her sit up on her elbow, and he heard the noise again. The phone. He looked over at her clock, his eyes squinted as he read the red numbers; it was two in the morning.

Sydney answered the cordless by her bed. "Hello?"

Sydney looked over at Mac, mouthing "Lori" as she sat up. "What do you want, Lori?"

Mac sat up beside her, leaning into her so he could put his ear to the phone also.

"How'd ya like my remodeling job on your house?" She started laughing.

"Lori, what's wrong with you?"

"Nothing, you mousy, fat bitch. I have no idea why Mac is with you; we all know you aren't any good."

"Why don't you leave me alone?"

"Because I like torturing you."

"The cops were here; they took fingerprints and are running them."

"So, what are you going to do, cry?"

"No," Sydney said as she took a deep breath. She'd already stood up for herself; now was the time to back that up. "I'm going to put your sorry ass in jail."

"I'll kill you before I go to jail, do you hear me?!"

Mac took the phone away from Sydney. "You won't touch her," he said calmly.

"What's with you, Mac? You like fat bitches?"

"Lori, if you come anywhere near her, you'll deal with me. Do I make myself clear?" he asked, listening to silence before she slammed the phone down. Mac took the phone away from his ear as he pushed the off button. "It's all right, honey. I won't let her hurt you," he replied as he put an arm around her shoulders, bringing her closer to his side. Using his thumb on the hand that still held the phone, he dialed the police station.

"Officer John Monroe; it's concerning his cousin Sydney."

"Mac, what are you doing?" Sydney asked as she looked up at him.

"John, it's Mac. Lori just called here admitting to the damage and threatened to kill Sydney if she pressed charges."

"You heard the threat?" John asked.

"Yeah, I heard her."

"We're picking Lori up in the morning, When I told

them to match the ones from the house to Lori's prints in the system, it was a direct hit. Can you bring Sydney in at eight?"

"We'll be there."

"Mac, you better keep her safe, do you hear me?"

"Yeah, bye," Mac said, ending the conversation as he pushed the off button. "We're going down to the station in the morning, so you can swear out a complaint against your sister," he replied as he turned to look at her. "John said the prints match Lori's and they were picking her up in the morning anyways."

"Mac..."

"Honey, she's unstable and I won't let her hurt you," he said as he leaned down, brushing his lips across hers. "Let's get some sleep; we have to be up in a few hours." He rolled her onto her side with her back facing him, as he took her into his arms.

"Mac..."

"Shh," was all he said as he held her close.

CHAPTER 9

SYDNEY SAT AT THE detective's desk waiting; they'd already taken her statement with Mac signing on as a witness to what he had heard. She lifted her head when she heard yelling.

"You're my cousin; you can't do this to me. I hate you," Lori screamed, catching a glance of Sydney as they dragged her down to the booking room. "You bitch! I'll kill you! Do you hear me? I'll kill you! You're not my sister; you're a fat ugly bitch."

Sydney turned as she felt a hand rest on her shoulder to see Mac standing behind her.

"It's all right, honey. Come on, let's go home; we have a wedding to go to."

"Oh my God, that's right; your brother's wedding! I forgot, I forgot. I'm so sorry Mac, I..." she stumbled as she rose up out of the chair.

Mac pulled her into a hug. "It's all right, sweetheart. We have plenty of time. Come on, let's go get ready. Weddings are always fun; we can sit back and make fun of the drunks. Trust me, we'll have plenty of party-goers to choose from." He smiled as he led her out of the station.

~~*~~

Sydney wiped her eyes as the bride and groom kissed.

They looked so happy and it was such a lovely service. Mac stood beside his brother; he looked so happy, and damn, he was handsome in that tux.

"See. Lei tell you he look good in a monkey suit, eh?"

Sydney turned her head and smiled at the elderly lady. "Yes, you did."

"He should have cut hair."

"Actually, Ms. Lei, I like it long."

The old lady laughed. "Me too, but I must give a good ribbing about something."

Sydney chuckled as they waited. His family had been very receptive to her; they all smiled and made her feel welcome, especially when she'd recognized a few of his brothers from the office—it seemed they were all cops. Standing as the bride and groom walked down the aisle, Sydney glanced at the maid of honor as she slid her hand to the inside crook of Mac's arm.

He leaned down, whispering something in her ear, bringing smiles to both their faces.

Sydney lowered her gaze, and then back up. She was beautiful, bright red hair and an hourglass shape. No wonder Mac was still smiling at her.

"You see the dragon?" Lei asked.

"What?" Sydney asked looking down at Lei. "What dragon?"

"The green jealousy one," she said with a chuckle. "You have no worries, Mac bring you.

Warning her to stay away from you."

"Stay away from me?" Sydney asked with some confusion and then caught on to what Lei was saying. "Oh, you mean she's a lesbian," she said, and looked up as Mac and his friend walked down the aisle. Mac winked and smiled at her, which had her lips curving up in one also, and then she saw the redhead look at her and do the same.

"I tell you, Mac warns her, you are his," Lei chuckled.

"He better hurry up if he wants that to be true," she mumbled under her breath, causing Lei to laugh.

"Mac no hurry to do the horizontal mambo—he must like you a lot. Here, I give you a secret to help" She pulled Sydney down so she could whisper in her ear.

Sydney shot up. "You're kidding, that works?"

"You listen to an old lady; get you plenty of bedroom boom boom." She made a thrusting motion with her hips.

"Lei, stop giving my son's friend advice," came a feminine voice.

"Why? Work for you." She smiled.

"Hi, I'm Mac's mother, Beth."

Sydney held her hand out and they shook. "I'm Sydney; it's a pleasure to meet you."

"You, too. What say we go congratulate the happy couple?" She took Sydney's hand.

Sydney went through the receiving line, being towed and introduced to everyone by Beth. When she got to Mac, he grabbed her away from his mother, pressing his lips to hers as he turned them away from everyone, his arms wrapping around her waist.

"Whatever she tells you, ignore it,"

"Why?"

"Hey man, you're causing a line to form," came a masculine voice.

"So what." Mac held her close, arms around her in a full body hug, his cheek resting against her head.

"Sydney, this is my cousin Marc; he's a lady's man, so stay away from him."

Marc grinned, winking at Sydney as the maid of honor stepped up. "Damn, does that mean me too?" she asked with a big smile.

Sydney's eyes moved to the redhead smiling at her. "Sorry, I'm a one-man woman," she said, as the redhead thrust her lips out in a pout.

"All right, you guys and girls," Beth said as she took hold of Sydney's arm again. "Stop what you're doing. Mac brings a nice girl around and you're going to scare her off. Come on, Sydney, you're safe with me."

"Don't take her too far, Mom," Mac replied as he released her, his fingers gliding down her body to her hips, where he squeezed gently before laying his hands there.

"I'll take her with me in the car if you don't behave. Really, Mac, bringing her here on the back of your bike."

"She likes the bike," he said with a smile as his mother led her away to a group of family members.

After the receiving line, Mac walked up behind Sydney, wrapping his arms around her waist, pulling her back up against him, and felt her melt into him. "Are we ready to go?" he asked, as she looked back at him over her shoulder.

"You are going to the reception, aren't you?" Beth asked.

"Yes."

"Why don't you let Sydney ride with your father and me in the car?"

Mac looked down at Sydney. "Do you want to go in the car?" he asked.

"It doesn't matter," Sydney said.

Mac leaned down to whisper in her ear. "Ride with me." His lips turning up with a smile, as Sydney trembled from the hotness of his breath against the sensitive skin of her neck.

"Mac, what are you doing?" Beth asked.

Lifting his head, Mac smiled. "Asking her to ride with me."

Beth's eyes narrowed. "Right."

"What? That's all I did." He gave her an innocent look.

"Uh huh, and just how did you ask? Because I don't think she'd be blushing if you were behaving yourself."

"She's a good girl, Mom; she blushes at everything." He smiled.

"If it's anything you say, no wonder she blushes," Beth said, causing the people standing with them to chuckle.

Mac picked Sydney up off her feet. "All right, that's enough. If you keep going, you may scare her away; we'll see you at the reception." He walked away from the group.

Sydney was chuckling. "You can put me down," she said, as they approached his bike.

"No way, then they might converge again," he replied as he listened to her laughter. Setting her down on her feet he turned her, lowering his mouth to hers. God, he loved the soft feel of her lips. Sliding the tip of his tongue along her bottom lip, he dipped it in as her lips parted for him.

"Mac," called out a male voice.

Mac and Sydney turned to a man walking up to them.

"Hey man," Mac said as they clasped hands. "Sydney, this is my brother Gabe."

Sydney looked at him. "Are you a cop?" she asked.

Gabe glanced to Mac and then back at her. "Yes."

"I thought I've seen you around the courthouse. You work at the seventh precinct with my cousin John."

"Monroe- yeah, now I remember you. He pointed you

out real fast one time when we were headed into court. Nice to meet you."

"You too."

"We better get going; we have to be there to walk in before Mitch and Celia," Mac said, as he put both hands on her waist and lifted her onto the bike.

Sydney folded both hands and placed them in front of her, so her dress wouldn't ride up.

"Are you going to the reception, Gabe?" she asked as Mac seated himself on the bike.

"Yeah, I'll see you there." He waved and turned around at someone calling his name.

Mac put his sunglasses on and turned around to look at her. "Ready, honey?"

"Yes." She wrapped both arms around him.

Mac leaned back, kissing her quickly. "All right, hold on." He put the bike in motion.

Beth smiled as Gabe walked back over to her. "He looks so happy with her."

"Yeah," Gabe replied as he turned; the bike disappeared down the road. "Too bad it'll be over soon."

"Gabe, what's going on?" Beth asked as she turned to see her other son approaching.

"You know he can't tell you, Mom," Jake said as he leaned down and placed a kiss on her cheek.

"I know, I know." She said with a wave of her hand. "Let's get going before we're late."

~~*~~

After the wedding party was introduced everyone sat down to enjoy the meal being served. Sydney looked around the table at Mac's family—they were so full of life; his two brothers, his mom and Lei sat around Mac and herself talking up a storm. The only time she enjoyed times like this was at her aunt's house during the holidays.

"Are you all right, honey?" Mac whispered in her ear.

Sydney smiled as she turned to him. "Yes, I'm just enjoying your family."

Mac leaned forward, placing a light kiss on her lips as his emotions warred with each other.

"Well, I wouldn't try to steal anything from this table with all you cops sitting here," came an elderly voice.

Everyone except Sydney shot Mac a look. Calmly, he turned to Celia's great-aunt. "Not all of us are cops, Miss Ellie," he said, as her brow furled up in concentration.

"I thought Celia said that all of Mitch's brothers were cops."

"No, one bar owner included," he said.

"Ellie, you must be thinking of Marc, Mitch's cousin," Beth said.

"Must be. The brain forgets at my age, children. Remember that," she said with a smile.

"Who wants to dance with a senile old lady and make her day?" she asked.

"I think I'll take that pleasure." Gabe grinned as he rose up out of his chair, escorting her to the dance floor.

Mac turned to Sydney. "Would you like to dance, madam?" he asked, as he held his hand out.

The thoughts that entered Sydney's mind took a back corner as she smiled at Mac placing her hand in his. "I'd love to," she said, letting him escort her to the dance floor, where he held her in his embrace, taking the lead as they slow-danced, his head lowering.

"Have I told you how beautiful you look?" he asked.

Sydney chuckled. "Only about a hundred times." She turned her head slightly inward to lay her cheek on his shoulder and met his gaze.

Mac smiled. "Then make it one hundred and one." He lowered his head, hers lips parted, a small sigh of pleasure escaped as he traced her bottom lip with his tongue.

Lowering his head a fraction more so they were covered from prying eyes, her back and his shoulder on one side, his shoulder and hair on the other, he continued to kiss her. His lips parted hers with an open-mouthed kiss, as his hand came up to cup the side of her face as he deepened the kiss.

"Ah, hey bro, the song's over; let her up for some air," Gabe said.

"I think we have our next family wedding to attend," Celia said as Mitch laughed.

Mac lifted his head, smiling down at Sydney. "Think they're cute, don't they?" he asked and watched her smile.

"I think I'll steal this dance," Marc said as they came apart, taking Sydney by the arm, pulling her into his embrace.

"Be nice." She said, as he twirled her around the dance floor.

"Watch her right hook," Mac called out loud, causing everyone to laugh.

"I think you better let up, don't you?" Jake asked, as he grabbed Mac by the arm and led him over to the bar.

"Back off, little brother."

"Back off? Jesus, Mac, she's business," he hissed as Gabe and Mitch walked up.

"I know," he hissed back. "And I also know what I'm doing, so back off."

"I hope to God you do. Because if this blows up in our faces because you can't keep your hands off her…"

"Jake, calm down," Gabe said.

"Yeah, I trust him to know how to handle it," Mitch said, slapping Mac on the shoulder.

"Yeah, Jakey boy. By the way, weren't you the one who told me to screw her, just to keep her near me?" Mac hissed out at his brother.

"All right boys, I don't know what this gathering is about, but the song is about to stop and Sydney is looking this way," Beth said as she came to stand between her boys.

Sydney walked up to the bar slowly; for some reason her stomach turned. If she looked up, people would be outright staring at her and turn away when she looked their way. Maybe it was because of the kissing, but how would they know? They could have been talking, for all these people could see.

"Hey, honey, Marc didn't get frisky, did he?" Mac asked as she came to stand beside him.

"No, I threatened to belt him if his hands wandered," she answered as she turned to Beth. "Could you tell me where the ladies room is, please?"

"Sure, Sydney. Its right around that corner." Beth pointed to the side of them.

"Thank you," she said and turned to Mac. "I'll be right back."

"She's sensing something's not right," Beth said as she looked up at her son.

"Yeah, I noticed that during the ceremony," he replied.

Beth gave him a sad smile. "She likes you."

"I know," he whispered. "I think it's time we left. I

don't want her here when people start getting tipsy. They might open their mouths by mistake."

"I think that's a wise idea." When Sydney walked back to the bar, he put his arm around her waist. "What do you say we leave?" he asked her.

Sydney looked up at him in surprise. "So soon?"

"I think he wants you alone, Sydney." Beth smiled.

"Oh, well in that case."

"Bye, Mom." Mac leaned down to kiss Beth on the cheek.

"Drive safe," she said, as she hugged Sydney.

"Always do." He led Sydney to the door.

~~*~~

Sydney opened her door, turning back to look at Mac, his eyes riveted on her. "Are you coming in?"

Mac looked down at her for a moment, the war within him losing as he lowered his head, covering her mouth with his as he thrust his tongue into her mouth.

Sydney moaned, wrapping her arms around his neck as he moved them into her apartment, shutting the door with his foot.

Running her hands down his back, she broke her mouth away, gasping for air, and groaned when his mouth landed on her neck. Her hands ran up to his chest, fingers undoing the buttons on the tux jacket. Sydney sighed. His pecs moved as she ran her hands over them.

Mac straightened slightly, when his cell phone rang.

Sydney grabbed it out of the inner pocket and answered. "Mac is busy," she said, hitting the end button and tossing the phone to the couch.

"That could have been important."

CHAPTER 10

"This is more important," she breathed, grabbing him by the front of his shirt.

Mac groaned as she took his mouth possessively, the kiss turning to an aggressive mating of mouths. Tossing his jacket, his hands slid to her rear, pulling her up against his hardness.

"Bedroom," he muttered, before lowering his mouth back down to hers as he moved them in that direction. His fingers found the zipper on the back of her dress and lowered it down to her hips, while Sydney's worked on his shirt buttons. When they stepped into the bedroom, Mac pulled away long enough to pull the shirt over his head and toss it.

Sydney ran her fingers across his chest, feeling his muscles contract beneath them.

"Sydney." He groaned, his voice thick with want.

Sydney brought her gaze up to his. "I want you, Mac." She said softly as she leaned forward, her lips touching the middle of his chest.

"God, honey. I want you, too," he said, before claiming her mouth with his. Bringing his hands up, he leisurely moved the dress off her shoulders, lips kissing and nipping her silken flesh, guiding the material down to her hips, past them until it fell in a puddle at her feet and then guided her over to the bed.

Sydney kicked her shoes off as she lowered her hands to his pants' button, undoing it as he unhooked her bra and slid it off.

"God, Sydney, you're beautiful," he said, looking down at her breasts. His hands traveled up from her waist until they rested beneath each mound. He watched as her nipples tightened in anticipation and lifting one thumb, he ran it lightly over one tip, listening to her moan as it hardened even more. Lowering his head, Mac ran his tongue over the turgid peak, and listened to her gasp of pleasure as her fingers tightened in his hair. His tongue swirled around nipple before he sucked her into his mouth, suckling and nipping while his other hand found its twin.

Sydney opened heavily lidded eyes, panting as he laved her breast. Her body trembled as his tongue circled her glistening nipple, before drawing it once more into the warmth of his mouth, teeth nipping.

When he looked up and saw her watching, Mac lifted his mouth with a smile and took hers again.

Sydney felt him lower her onto the bed, his thigh coming up to rest right between hers. Moving against his thigh, she felt the dampness from her slide over her panties, and with a moan brought her hand up to his hardness, rubbing her palm against the rigid shaft.

Mac let out a groan as he pulled his mouth away from hers. "God, Sydney," he whispered, as he thrust his erection against her wandering palm, then backed up so his fingers could find her panties. Inch by inch he took them off her, placing kisses along the way as he went. When he stood at the end of the bed, his gaze kept hers as he took a foil packet out of the pocket, before he pushed his pants and boxer briefs down.

Crawling back on to the bed, he pressed light kisses and nips to her thigh, slowly working up to her stomach, his tongue leaving trails as he worked his way up, one of his hands trailing as his fingers sought out her heat. His cock jumped and she trembled as he cupped her trimmed thatch, his finger sliding between her damp folds, and she arched against him with a moan as he slipped a long finger deep inside.

Mac's mouth sought her breast, taking the other nipple into his mouth as his fingers parted her more, his thumb finding her clit. Her muscles tightened around his digits as she bucked under him. "You're so wet," he murmured huskily as he covered her mouth with his.

When he pulled away, Sydney met his gaze, afraid he was stopping, until he tore open the foil packet and placed the condom on his erection. When he came back down, she opened her legs and he slid between them, covering her mouth. With his lips?

Shivers shot through her as his cock nudged her entrance. She moved her legs up his sides.

Mac entered her with a slow, short thrust; he knew that it had been awhile since she'd had sex, and didn't want to hurt her. After going forward an inch, he withdrew, lubricating himself with her essence, and entered her again just as slow. He could feel her inside walls closing around him, her breathing heavy as she stretched to accommodate him; God, she was so tight, like taking a virgin without having to deal with the hymen. Lifting his mouth from hers, he kissed the side of her neck. "God, honey, you feel so good." He pushed in all the way.

C. A. Salo

"So do you." Her nails biting into his back, pussy tightening as she arched up.

Mac brought his head back up, taking control of her mouth again as he started thrusting in and out of her, loving the way she responded.

"Oh God," Sydney panted as she broke her mouth away from his, her hands going to his bottom, pushing when he thrust into her, grinding herself against him, causing him to groan as he thrust into her deep and hard the next time. Sydney matched his rhythm, moving her fingers from his bottom up his slick back until they tangled in his hair.

Gasping, she kissed him hard, her tongue thrusting to meet his as he moved his hand between them, his knuckle skimming over her engorged clit.

"M-Mac!" she yelled, as she tore her mouth away from his. "O-oh God."

He watched her eyes flutter as her orgasm hit. Removing his hand, he lifted himself slightly and thrust into her again and again, his pelvis grinding against her swollen nub. He felt the aftershocks going through her body. Picking up the pace, he felt his balls tighten as he reached his own release, groaning when he thrust into her the last time, settling himself deep as he exploded. He shook once before collapsing on top of her, his head coming to rest between her breasts.

Sydney, still in a daze, brought her hand up and ran it over his slick back, shivering as an aftershock worked its way through her when he lifted himself above her.

Mac leaned down, pressing a tender kiss her to her swollen lips. "Are you okay?" he asked, as her eyes fluttered open.

"Yes, are you?"

Mac smiled and kissed her again. "Yes," he whispered. "I'm fine. I have to go to the bathroom; I'll be back in a minute."

Sydney sat up with the sheet around her; rising, she headed to the bathroom also.

Mac leaned down, kissing her softly when he came out, stepping aside so she could go in. Leaning against the wall, he had no problem standing there naked as he waited.

When she came back out he smiled, took a hold of her hand, and led her back to the comfort of her bed.

Wondering if what they had done was right, Mac lay in bed holding her, listening to her even breathing. Sure felt right enough. Too right. With a sigh he tightened his arms around her as he closed his eyes. He'd deal with it later, but not tonight. Tonight was special; tonight he felt something he hadn't felt in a very long time.

~~*~~

Sydney's eyes barely opened as she lavished in the warmth surrounding her.

"Why is it whenever I wake up, you're always on top of me?"

Lifting her head, she stared down at Mac's smiling face. "You're comfortable."

Tightening his arms around her, Mac lifted his head, placing a kiss on her lips as he scooted her on top of him, her legs resting on either side of his hips.

Sydney gasped when his erection rubbed against her clit, and lifted her gaze to his.

Trailing his fingers from her thighs up her waist to her breasts, Mac lifted his gaze from her breasts to her eyes, lifted one hand to the back of her neck, bringing her mouth down to his.

Sydney moved her arms so they rested on either side of his head, as his mouth sensuously moved over hers, her hair falling around them like a soft curtain.

Mac's hands came up to the sides of her face, holding her while his mouth ravaged hers, his thumbs near the corners of her mouth, tilting her head the way he wanted, controlling the kiss when she went to speed it up. When Sydney surrendered to his mouth, her body melted, she ground her clit against his erection. Changing the kiss back to a soft openmouthed tangle, his gaze met hers. "I need to get my pants," he murmured huskily.

Sydney nodded. His eyes followed her sweet little body as she backed up to the end of the bed and grabbed his pants off the floor. His gaze slid down as her breasts played hide and seek behind her hair, a groan escaped his parted lips with the tightening of his groin.

Sydney grabbed the foil packet out of his pocket and scooted back up the bed, sitting on his thighs, as he stroked his substantial erection. Lifting her hand, she stroked him with her finger from the base to the tip, a cat-like smile on her face when he jumped beneath her and brought her gaze back up to his.

Mac growled, grabbed for the condom, but she lifted it away from him and tore it open, taking the condom out. After looking at it for a second, she started unrolling it onto his erection, causing him to breathe deeply with the sensations of her fingers sliding down his length.

When Sydney finished rolling the condom on, she leaned over, pressing a featherlight kiss on the middle of his chest before working her way up over one male nipple. When she nipped it with her teeth, she smiled as he grunted on an exhaled breath, and then she moved up to his shoulder and to his neck until she reached his mouth.

Mac's hands traveled her body. When she found his mouth, he put his hands on her hips and lifted her so he could guide himself inside her hot, wet sheath until he was buried deep within her warmth.

Sydney moaned as his thickness stretched her, eyes fluttering shut as her lips parted, sighing with the incredible sensations of just having him in her. With the guidance of his hands on her hips, she started moving on top of him, picking up the rhythm. Lifting her mouth off his, she breathed deeply.

Mac suckled a taut nipple, as his other played with its twin. Moving his hands back down her sides to her waist, he pushed up into her as she lowered herself.

"Oh God, Mac." Sydney panted, the excitement of an orgasm beginning, working its way through her body. Never in her life had she felt so utterly horny, and she loved it.

Mac was surprised she was ready to orgasm so soon. Typically, it took some time to build a woman up. Then again, he was ready to go the minute he woke up next to her. Moving one hand between them, his thumb slid between her swollen wet folds to find her nub and he listened to her moan as he thrust up into her.

Sydney started to shake, her inside walls convulsing around his engorged member. When she cried out his name, he moved his hands to her waist and kept up the rhythm they had started as she slowed with the force of her release. Mac thrust up into her again and again until he buried himself deep, groaning as he erupted with his own release.

Sydney slid down, collapsing on his chest, her hands resting next to his on the bed.

Mac shook with an aftershock as his fingers entwined with hers. After a few moments, he kissed the side of her head.

Sydney raised her head.

"Good morning."

"You make me feel good," she whispered.

"Hmm, that's me. Mister Feel Good." He smiled as he rolled over, pinning her beneath him. "I have to go clean up; that's one thing I hate about condoms." He kissed her one more time before moved off her and going to the bathroom.

Sydney yanked the sheet over herself and closed her eyes; the area between her thighs still throbbed.

"Hey, you're not falling back to sleep, are you?" Mac asked, as he stood over her.

Sydney stretched out like a lounging cat. "I'm thinking about it." Her hand lowered the sheet from her head as her eyes fluttered open.

"If you want to jump in the shower, I'll start the coffee." He sat down next to her, brushing some hair out of her face.

"Um, all right," she said as she sat up. "But you have to join me after you start it."

Mac leaned over and kissed her. "I'd love to, but I'm out of condoms."

"I'm not; I bought some after the door thing."

"The door thing?"

"Yeah, when you had me against the front door."

"Ah yes, the door," he said as he kissed her again. "All right, honey. I'll meet you in the shower." He rose up off the bed and headed for the kitchen. How she could be ready to go again in such a short amount of time amazed him. That's why he'd brought three condoms, figured he wouldn't need more than that; it wasn't that he lacked in that area, hell, he was as horny as the next guy. What he hadn't figured on was Sydney's effect on him.

~~*~~

Sydney sat at her table sipping her cup of hot coffee. She had certainly never taken a shower like that before, and she trembled, remembering the things he had done to her body. Hearing him behind her, she took another quick sip.

"So where do you shop for clothes?"

"Clothes?"

"Yeah, for work."

"Oh, um. Well, I haven't been shopping in a while; maybe I should go to the mall."

"That sounds about right. When are we leaving?" he asked, as he took a sip of his own coffee.

"You want to go with me?"

"Sure, why not."

"Well, you're a guy," she snorted.

Mac grinned. "Glad you noticed."

"I thought men hated shopping worse than me," she replied, as his eyebrow arched, sending her muscles between her thighs clenching. "All right, but we take my car."

"What's wrong with the bike?"

"I have to buy more than one outfit. How am I supposed to hang on to everything and you on your bike?"

"Good point. Okay, your car it is, but I drive."

"Why do you have to drive?"

"Because I like to feel in control of my vehicle."

"You called my car a hunk of junk," Sydney complained, as she set both mugs in the sink.

"I did, didn't I. I'm still driving." Mac grinned.

"Fine, you drive." Turning, she grabbed the keys, handing them to him, yelping when he swatted her butt on the way out.

~~*~~

They spent two hours at the mall, going through what seemed like a hundred stores. "I didn't realize it would take this long," Mac groaned as they walked down the mall.

"Are you complaining?" Sydney asked with a smile, as she tilted her head up toward him.

"No, but I thought you said you didn't like to shop. You sure as hell looked like a pro to me." He put his arm around her shoulders, drawing her closer.

"Hey, it's not that easy. I haven't bought work clothes in two years. They changed all the styles on me, so I had to try them on and see how they fit."

"I could have helped with that if you would have let me in the dressing room with you."

Sydney slapped his arm. "And how would I explain that to the attendant?"

"Easy, that I'm your fashion advisor and have to help you zip up the backs of the dresses."

"And I'm sure she would have believed that."

Mac chuckled as he swung her around to face him, planting a kiss on her in the middle of the mall. Catching something out of the corner of his eye, he pulled her into the jewelry store they were standing in front of.

Sydney looked up at him, confused. "Mac?"

He stopped in front of the diamond case, smiling up at the sales girl. "I'd like to see a two carat solitaire, flawless or better, with an S1 or higher rating set in platinum, please."

"Mac, what are you doing?" Sydney whispered.

Mac leaned down to her ear. "Chang," was all he whispered, his tongue playing with her lobe as the saleslady handed the ring to him to look at. Straightening Mac took her hand, slipping the shiny rock onto her ring finger. "What do you think of this one, honey?"

CHAPTER 11

"Mac."

Mac turned away from Sydney. "Chang, how are you?" he asked, as they shook hands.

"Fine. You buy ring for your woman?"

"Yes, we're looking; show him the ring, honey," Mac said.

Sydney kept her eyes lowered as she held up her hand.

Sydney almost flinched when Chang put his fingers under hers to lift her hand and inspect the ring.

"Nice choice. So my offer is out, then?" Chang asked as he released her hand.

Slipping his hand around her waist, Mac brought her closer to him. "Sorry, Chang. She's too special to me," he said.

Sydney's heart jumped at that, as a smile touched her lips.

"Good. About time you have some luck with women." Chang smiled as he snapped his fingers.

Mac watched as the man behind him handed a card to the sales lady. "Put it on my account," Chang said.

"But sir, that is a very expensive ring," she stammered.

"No price too high for my friend."

"Chang, I can't accept that," Mac stated.

"Yes, you good friend to me, Mac; consider it my wedding present. I will not be able to attend ceremony, however, seeing as how I will be leaving for China soon, and stay there for awhile."

"Problems?" he asked, as he kept his expression under control at that news.

"Not yet, this is why I leave," he said with a smile. "You may raise your eyes, woman," he said.

Sydney glanced to Mac for confirmation. When he nodded, she raised her gaze to look at Chang.

"You are lucky to have a good man such as Mac. When you marry, you need not keep eyes lowered when we next meet," he said with a smile, as he took his card back from the saleslady. "My mistresses are waiting; may many children come your way." He turned on his heel, leaving the store.

Sydney looked up at Mac. "What are we going to do now?"

"Why, get married; do you have your date picked out yet? If not, I have a great calendar in the back for you to look at." The salesgirl smiled as she handed Mac the receipt.

"Thanks, but we're all set," he said, taking a hold of Sydney's hand, leading her out of the mall.

As soon as they were both in the car, Sydney took the ring off and handed it to him.

"What's this for?"

"What am I supposed to do with it?"

"Wear it."

"Wear it? We're not engaged."

"No, but if Chang happens to run into us again, he'll wonder where it is," he said, handing it back to her and watching as she put it back on. "It does look good, doesn't it?" he asked as he lifted her hand, his lips brushing the tops of her knuckles.

Mac helped her unload and put away her new purchases once they were back at her apartment. While they'd been gone, the landlord had the window fixed and left a note saying he'd get in touch with her about installing an alarm system, which made Mac breath a bit easier.

"Do you want to stay for dinner?" Sydney asked, as she walked into the living room.

"I should get to the Mer-Fay; Walt's probably wondering where the hell I am."

"Hey, your phone hasn't rung all day," she said, as she went over to the fridge, taking out stuff for a salad. "It'll take me seven minutes to make it," she said, as she took some chicken tenders out and then closed the door, opening the freezer to grab a box.

Mac's eyebrows went up. "Seven minutes?"

"Yeah, I'm the best fast cooker you'll ever see." She smiled as she put everything down on the counter, and bent to look for a frying pan in the bottom cabinet.

Mac's gaze followed her bottom when she bent over and walked up behind her, cupping her butt cheeks with his hands. "Maybe dinner can wait," he said as she straightened up, his hands moving up to her waist as he moved her backward, until her bottom pressed up against the hardness straining the front of his jeans.

"Mac," she moaned. She laid her hands on the counter for leverage when he ground his hips against her, his hands moving up to cup her breasts from behind.

"I want you, Sydney," he whispered in her ear, causing

her to tremble. His fingers moved to her jeans button, popping it, the back of his fingers sliding down soft bare skin as he pulled the zipper down. His head lowered; hot breath causing her to shiver as he placed a gentle kiss on her neck, and then his cell phone rang.

Without moving his hand from her damp hot groin, he grabbed his cell, pushing the on button. "I'm busy," he growled, hitting the end button he put the phone on the counter, bringing his hand back to her waist he started sliding her pants and panties down. "I hope you appreciate that," he said as he took her earlobe between his teeth.

"I do." She panted, reaching one hand around to grab his butt cheek. She listened to his heavy breathing in her ear, her body trembling, pussy clenching as he slid his hand down to the hotness between her legs.

"Here?"

"No, the door."

"Can't make it that far. Wall." Swinging her around, Mac attacked her mouth, listening to her moan; he backed her up against the wall and slid her pants off before reaching for his own. He felt her reach in his back pocket and grab a condom before they hit the floor. Taking it away from her trembling fingers, he made quick work of putting it on, before lifting her against the wall and settling himself between her thighs, as she wrapped her legs around him and felt something break within him. Growling, he met her passion-glazed eyes as he thrust up, his hands pushing her hips down as he gripped the tender flesh.

Sydney moaned as he entered her with an urgency she hadn't felt in him before, her hands on his shoulders holding on as he pumped into her. Lowering her mouth, she captured his and took it with a ferocity he had never had with a woman. Lowering one hand, he found her nub with his fingers. "Mine," he growled. "You're mine."

Sydney was teetering right on the edge as he spoke, tore her mouth away from his. "Oh God, yes," she cried as her orgasm started, his words pushing her off the edge.

Mac kept pumping into her. "Come on, honey. I love it when you orgasm." His voice husky, he could feel her insides contracting around him, trying to milk him of his seed as she cried out his name when her second orgasm hit hard. Mac thrust into her two more times before he took his own release, roaring her name.

Sydney laid her head on his shoulder, her hot breath hitting the side of his neck.

Mac held on to her as their bodies trembled with the aftershocks of the mind-blowing orgasms they both had. He wondered where and when in the hell taking her became a primal one. Need? One moment he was fine, the next he'd gone caveman and nothing would ease him but her.

"I didn't know it was possible to orgasm like that," she whispered against his neck.

"Me neither, honey. Hold on," he said, as he pushed away from the wall, holding her tightly he carried to the bathroom.

~~*~~

Mac walked into the Mer-Fay, and noticed Walt look up at him as he sat down at the end of the bar.

Walt dropped a soda in front of him. "So how was the wedding?"

"The wedding was great."

"And after the wedding?"

"Even better," Mac answered as he looked up. "Don't

even say it," he said raising his hand to stop his next words. "I heard it from Jake, Gabe and Mitch on my way over here, one by one."

"I trust you," was all Walt said, as he walked to the other end of the bar.

~~*~~

The next day, Sydney was reading over some paperwork when Tamara stopped in front of her. "I see something new," she said, and Sydney looked up, smiling.

"Huh, oh yeah. I had to replace all of my work clothes; Lori ruined all of them."

"I'm not talking about that; I'm talking about that." Tamara pointed to her finger.

Sydney looked down and saw the engagement ring on her finger; she had forgotten to take it off this morning. "Oh, it was a gift," she said, hiding her hand under the desk.

"Oh no, you don't." Tamara said, reaching for her hand and bringing it back up. "That is some rock; moving a little too fast, aren't you? You've known him for what-three, four weeks?"

"It's not like that," Sydney said, and proceeded to tell Tamara the story about Chang.

"Chang? He's a drug lord," Tamara said. "What kind of business is Mac into?"

"Not that. He said he used to have dealings with him a long time ago."

"If I were you I'd take it easy with this guy. Once you're in it, you're very lucky if you get out alive." She walked back to her office.

Sydney looked down at the ring as her stomach turned.

She wanted to believe Mac, but she also knew that what Tamara had said was right also. When it came right down to it, she didn't know much about him; he had told her there were things he couldn't tell her about yet, but he'd promised that he hadn't been doing anything illegal with Chang. Elbows on desk, she covered her face with her hands, a heavy sigh escaping her parted lips as she thought about what to do. He was good to her, his family was great, and he was damn good in bed. She didn't think with so many cops as brothers he'd do anything illegal. Sydney snorted. Yeah, right. Look at Lori.

Cops, his brother's and cousin, Marc. Getting up from her seat she went to Tamara's office. "I'm going to lunch," she said, as she headed out the door.

She had no idea she was being watched as she walked the two blocks to the police station. "Is Officer John Monroe here?" she asked the Sergeant sitting at the desk.

"I think so. And you are?"

"Sydney Ripley, his cousin," she replied, going to sit on the bench when he motioned her that way.

"Syd, what's up?" John asked, as he stepped into the foyer.

Sydney got up and walked over to him. Taking him by the elbow, she led him away from prying ears. "Mac has a cousin on the force, here in this station and brothers. I'm not sure where they are, but um, I don't know how to ask this, but is there any way you can run a background check on Mac, to see if he's done anything illegal or if he's helped his brothers on a case or anything?" she whispered.

"About time you get your head out of your ass?" John snorted as he stepped back, his thumbs hooking onto the inside of his belt.

"John, don't. I just need to know if he has anything to do with a guy named Chang," she whispered, as his brows furrowed.

"You're talking Mr. 'I'm the biggest drug lord in the city' Chang?"

"Yes. Can you do it?"

"Why and where the hell did you get that rock?" John asked, picking up her hand when he noticed the sparkle coming off her finger.

Sydney shook his grip loose. "Can you?"

"Sydney, his cousin works here; if I start poking around he'll want to know why."

"I know." Biting her bottom lip, she moved as her wide eyes kept John's. "Have you heard anything?"

God, he hated doing this to her, especially with the vulnerable way she was looking at him right now, but he'd tried warning her away, and now his hands were tied. "No, not about Mac being involved with anything like that, and if there was a sting going on, the department would be buzzing."

"Can you find out for me?"

John ran a hand through his hair. "It could take a couple of days. Maybe more, but I'll see what I can find out."

"Thanks, John," she said, kissing him on the cheek.

John watched as she walked out before he went back to Marc, who in turn picked up the phone and made a call. Standing there, he watched, watched what his betrayal to his cousin looked like.

~~*~~

"Mac."

"It's Marc; your little sweetheart was just in here asking

for a background check on you, and to see if you've helped with any cases detailing Chang."

"Yeah, I already got a call."

"What are you going to do?"

"I'm not sure."

"Damn it man, don't let this blow up in our faces. Do your brothers know?"

"Yeah, don't worry; business will be done by the end of the week."

"You had better be sure. Keep her on a leash and tell Chang, nice rock."

Mac hit the end button as he opened his door. "Walt!" he yelled down the stairs. "We have a problem."

CHAPTER 12

SYDNEY WAS UNEASY THE rest of the day, like she had done something wrong. "It's just nerves." She walked down the sidewalk. Sydney stopped, turning to look behind her, searching for something. "You're paranoid," she mumbled, as she continued down the sidewalk.

"Hey honey, need a ride?" Mac asked, as he pulled up alongside her, his brow arching when she kept walking.

"Sydney," he said with a raised voice, watching her turn as her hand flew up to her chest.

"My God, Mac. I didn't hear you." She walked over to him.

"Are you all right?"

"Yeah, I'm okay," she said, as she seated herself behind him.

Mac parked the bike next to her car. He got off and helped her, and as they walked to her door, she dug around in her purse for her keys and opened the door.

Following her inside, he watched her as she set her purse on the counter and walked into the kitchen.

"Sydney, are you all right?" he asked, as she started taking things out of the fridge.

"I told you I was."

"You seem quiet. Bad day at work?" he asked, leaning back on the counter.

"No, Mac. You said you had dealings with Chang. You didn't do anything illegal, did you?" she asked, looking up at him.

"No why?"

"It's been bothering me. You do know he's a drug lord or something, right?"

"Yes, I know what he does."

"And you haven't-gotten into that, have you, I mean drugs?" she asked, her stomach churning, fingers fisting, fidgeting as she awaited his answer.

"No, I've never dealt in drugs; why a bunch of questions all of a sudden?"

"Because- well I- what did you do for him?"

"Information. He needed to know some things and was referred to me to get it."

"That's all, and it wasn't anything illegal, right?"

"No, Sydney, it wasn't anything illegal. I've told you that before."

"You also told me that there were things you couldn't tell me, and I, I just have this uneasy feeling sitting in my gut."

Mac pulled her into his arms. "Then let it set easy. I have never done anything illegal in my adult life." He lowered his mouth to hers. He had to get her off this line of questioning and fast.

"I still feel like there's something important you're not telling me." She said, when he lifted his head.

Mac cupped the side of her face. "Honey, I will tell you everything in time," he said, as he brushed his lips across hers again, getting a better response from her the second time.

Zack

"How about I help you fix one of those seven minute dinners?"

Swiftly making dinner, Mac helped her clean up and then pulled her into his arms.

"How about I help you get into something a little more comfortable?" he asked, as he walked her backward toward the bedroom.

Sydney wrapped her arms around his neck. "How comfortable?" She kissed his neck.

Mac ran his hands up her sides and to her back, unzipping her dress. "Naked comfortable," he mumbled as he got them into the bedroom, sliding her dress down.

Sydney pulled his t-shirt out of his jeans, lifting it up and over his head. "I think I like that idea," she said as her fingers unsnapped the button on his jeans. Everything was going to be all right, she thought, as her hands moved over him. She could sense he wasn't lying to her about doing illegal stuff, but there was still something big he wasn't telling her. With any luck, John would have some answers for her tomorrow and she'd be able to laugh her paranoia off.

"I thought you might." He took her mouth eagerly as he pushed her back on to the bed, following her down he made quick work of her panties and bra. Moving away, he sat up and shoved his jeans down.

Sydney watched his erection spring free and reached a hand forward, running her fingers up his shaft, helping him roll the condom on.

Mac caught her fingers. Moving her hands above her head, he held them there. "I'll explode if you keep doing that," he said, as he captured her mouth with his. He slid into her, listening to her moan as he did. It felt so right to be in her; they fit so well together, better than he'd ever felt.

Meeting her gaze, he stroked into her again and again, her hips arching toward him as he held her wrists to the bed. After thrusting into her several times, he felt her convulsing against him and lifted his mouth so he could watch her. Her eyes closed, her lips parted, and she cried his name as her release took hold of her. He thrust into her several more times, feeling the aftershocks course through her as his balls tightened. He took his own release as he groaned her name.

It was late by the time they lay spooned together holding each other. Mac had loved her several more times before he let her rest. He was half asleep when he heard her soft "I love you." Opening his eyes, he stared at the wall for a moment before he started loving her again, tenderly, getting his fill as if it were the last time he would ever touch her again, because if things happened the way they were supposed to, it was, and he wanted to remember everything about her.

~~*~~

Sydney woke up the next morning as her alarm went off. Stretching, she reached a hand over to feel empty sheets beside her, and opened her eyes to see that she was alone in bed. Getting up, she walked past the open bathroom door into the living room to find herself alone. Going into the kitchen, she saw a note propped up by the coffee pot.

Had to go, business. Mac.

Setting the note on the counter, she started the coffee pot before going to the bathroom to get ready for work.

The office was buzzing about something, but every time she came close enough to hear what was happening, things would stop. Walking up to Caitlin, the D.A.'s secretary, she asked her, "What's going on?"

Caitlin looked up at her. "What do you mean?"

"All the buzzing going on."

"Oh, just a case the D.A. is working on," she said, not looking up from her paperwork.

Sydney felt put off. "Oh, well. With any luck, whatever it is will settle down; all this buzzing is starting to sound like a beehive."

"I know what you mean."

Sydney kept her gaze on her for a moment before turning on her heel, heading back to her desk.

By the end of the day Sydney was bored and jumpy because whatever was happening, the office did not want her to know about it. Which made her feel left out. Tamara had been in meetings all day. She was the ADA's secretary and like Caitlin, she knew what was going on and why-except on this. Plus, John hadn't gotten back to her yet and with all the slow time she'd had today, her guilty conscience about going behind Mac's back kept sprouting up. Biting her bottom lip as she walked down the steps, she saw Mac waiting for her and she smiled for the first time that day. "Hey," she said, walking up to him.

"Hey honey, get on I'll take you home," He said, as he held out his hand to help her seat herself.

When they walked through the door, Sydney put her purse on the counter and turned to face him. "I have to tell you something."

"Sure, what's up?" he asked, leaning on the kitchen counter, looking at her.

"I, I um, talked to John yesterday and asked him to do something for me," she said, her voice lowering, hands twisting together. "I asked him t-to, run a b-background ch-check on you and see if you've ever helped out on a case for your brothers."

"You did?" he asked, tilting his head, as she nodded hers. "Why?"

"B-because of the Chang thing."

"I explained that."

"I-I know."

"So, you asked John to run a background check on me?"

"Mac, I..." she started as he held up a hand.

"I know, Marc called me. If you wanted to know something, Sydney, all you had to do was ask, but instead you call your cousin to do a little snoop and prowl. Thanks," he said, as he pushed away from the counter heading toward the door.

"Mac," she said, running up behind him. "Where are you going?"

"Leaving," he said, as he walked through the door.

Sydney stopped in the doorway. "P-please don't leave-Mac," she said, as he started his bike.

"Don't call me; I'll call you," he replied coldly, revving the motor, he took off.

Sydney shut the door with tears in her eyes. "What a great day." She leaned up against it. While it was a relief to get the background check off her chest, now she felt like crap because she'd hurt him. Not that it showed on his face; hell, his features went blank, showing no emotion at all and now he was mad at her. Hurt and mad. What a way to have a relationship, if she still had one. Sighing, she moved, swiping the tears as she ambled to the kitchen.

~~*~~

Zack

Sydney went to work the next day exhausted. She'd tossed and turned all night, with the worry of never hearing from Mac again. God, why did she have to be so stupid; why couldn't she just trust what he said and take it at that? He sounded so upset when he left yesterday, telling her not to call him. How was she supposed to apologize if he didn't want her calling? But then the tingle at the back of her mind wondered why he'd be so upset if he had nothing to hide.

"Hey, Sydney, you all right?" Tamara asked.

Sydney looked up from her desk. "Just peachy."

"Spill," Tamara said, sitting on the corner of her desk.

"I told Mac last night that I talked to John about running a background check on him, and to see if he'd helped his brothers out with Chang."

"Ah, and I take it he wasn't too happy."

"No, not happy at all," she said. "I'd rather not talk about it."

"All right," Tamara said getting up and walking back to her office.

A few hours later the phone rang, and Sydney answered it.

"It's Mac; how about I pick you up after work for dinner?"

"Yeah, sounds good." She smiled.

"See you then," he said and hung up.

~~*~~

Sydney walked down the steps of the courthouse to sit across the street on the park bench to wait. He wanted to have dinner with her so that was good, right? Maybe he wasn't very mad at her after all.

After sitting there for two hours, she started rethinking the mad part. The birds were starting to think she was a statue. Getting up, she looked down the dark sidewalk as she started home; he knew she hated walking after dark. Just as she crossed the street she heard a bike and turned. Her spirits sank when she saw that it wasn't Mac.

"Hey, Sydney."

"Hi, Brian."

"You need a ride?"

"No, I was just going home. Mac was supposed to meet me for dinner, but something must have happened." She said, not able to ignore the butterflies in her stomach.

"Mac's been at the Mer-Fay; I just left. You want a ride down there?"

Sydney lowered her gaze. "Would you mind?" she asked.

"No, Sydney. Hop on," he said as he held a hand out for her.

Sydney took his hand and seated herself behind him, one hand at his waist holding on, and took hold of the grab rail with the other.

Sydney had a bad feeling walking up to the door of the Mer-Fay. Brian was ahead of her and had already gone in, but for some reason she couldn't name, she couldn't shake the bad vibes running up her spine, leaving goose bumps on her arms. Her chest rose with a deep breath, and she let it out slowly, trying to calm herself as she opened the door and stepped in to the bar. Sydney noticed Walt look up at her and look away. Her eyes narrowed at that as she moved her gaze to the end of the bar and stood there frozen, her breath held deep in her lungs, cold tingles running over her arms and up to her brain as a rock hit her stomach, when she saw Mac standing there with a curvaceous blonde in his arms. Her mouth opened to say something, but nothing would come out as he lowered his lips to the side of her neck, his hands wandering over her bottom. Sydney went numb; she couldn't even say anything when he glanced up, his eyes meeting hers, her head tilting as hurt suffocated her.

Stumbling backward, she reached for the door. She didn't even remember walking outside, but she was, and she was walking down the street. It never hit her what kind of neighborhood she was walking through, when her foot caught on something and she fell. She put her hands out in front of her, and yelped when her hands and knees hit the pavement. She sat there stunned for a moment, before looking down at her hands. Her eyes were filled and blurry with tears, but she could still make out the blood on her one knee as it dripped down her leg.

Touching the cut with care, she sucked in her breath as she moved the torn nylon out of the way.

"Hey lady, you all right?"

"No," Sydney answered, as she looked up and saw a gun pointed at her.

"Too bad, it just got worst. Hand me that rock you got on your hand," he said, motioning the gun to her fingers.

Sydney's hand shook as she tried to take the ring off.

"Hurry up, lady," the guy yelled, as he hit the side of her face with his fist.

Crying out, Sydney fell sideways, lying on her purse as she felt him pull the ring off her finger. Wanting to cry out for him not to kill her, but hurting so emotionally already, she wasn't sure if she cared as he hit her again.

"Thanks, lady," he said, as he took off running.

Sydney lay there for a moment before getting up and stumbled as she tried to walk as fast as she could. Her legs felt like rubber, wobbling as she cried.

"Sydney, you all right?" Her neighbor asked.

"Yes," she said, hiding her face behind her hair as her hands shook, making it difficult to get the key in the lock.

"You sure? That knee looks bad."

"I'm fine, Kevin; I fell," she said, pushing her door open. "Um, what time is it?"

"Past ten. Are you sure you're all right?"

"Yes, thank you," she whispered. Stepping through the doorway, she shut and locked it. Crying out in relief, she stumbled to the sanctuary of her bathroom.

~~*~~

Sydney kept her head down at work all day; every time Tamara came by, she looked the other way.

"Want to tell me what's going on?" Tamara asked, as she stopped in front of her desk.

"Nothing."

"Come on Sydney, you've been quiet as a mouse all day and every time I walk by, you won't look up at me. Want to tell me why, and why you have your hair down today? That's not you and we both know it."

"I have a lot to do."

"Sydney, I'm your boss. Look up at me-now, Sydney," she said, and gasped when she saw the side of Sydney's face. "My God, what happened? Who did this to you?" she asked, as she eyed the bruise covering her face from the eye down.

"Someone mugged me last night."

"Mugged you? Did you call the police? What did they take?"

Sydney shook her head. "No, I didn't call them. All he took was the ring."

"Sydney, why didn't you call me?"

"Because I didn't want to be around anyone," she said. She lifted her hand to remove her glasses as tears started filling her eyes.

"What happened to your hands?"

"I fell when I was walking."

"Is that why you drove in this morning?"

"Yes."

"Did you go to the doctor?"

Sydney shook her head as she lowered it. "I don't want to talk about it."

"All right, let me know if you change your mind," Tamara said, as she walked to her office.

~~*~~

Mac sat at the end of the bar when Walt called his name. Looking up, he saw a kid no older than twenty-one walking toward him.

"You Mac?" the kid asked.

"And you are?"

"Yo, man. No need for that. I have something I want to get rid of and heard you were the man to ask."

"What is it?" Mac asked, watching as he pulled the ring out of his pocket and handed it to him, Mac felt his guts twisting. "Where'd you get this?" he asked, as his fist closed around the ring.

"Off some lady."

"When?" he yelled.

"Yo man, last night; she was walking on the road and fell, so I went to offer my help and helped myself to that little beauty."

Mac picked him up by his shirtfront. "Did you hurt her?" he yelled in his face.

"Man, what's up?"

"Did you hurt her?!" he yelled again, causing the people in his bar to look at them.

"I slammed her upside the head a couple times when she couldn't get it off fast enough."

Mac drew back his fist, punching the kid in the face. "What else did you do to her?!"

"Nothing man, she was already bleeding from falling," he said, and then grunted when Mac hit him again.

It took Walt and Greeley to pull Mac off him.

"Yo man, what's your problem?" the kid asked, wiping the blood from his nose.

"The problem is, you went after his woman," Greeley said, as Walt held Mac back.

"Sorry, man. Didn't know she was yours," he said, and backed up when Mac came at him again.

"I think you better get out of here, kid," Walt said over his shoulder, as Greeley push the kid out the door.

Mac slammed his fist on the bar. "Damn!" he shouted and then turned and walked to the stairs. He knew he should have sent someone to follow her as soon as she left last night. He thought she'd taken her car until Brian told him he'd picked her up in front of the courthouse, and by the time he'd sent two men out looking for her she was gone.

CHAPTER 13

OH, WHAT A HELL of a week it'd been, since she'd last seen Mac in the bar with the blonde attached to his front. Sighing, she glanced around. Everyone in the office was still clamming up around her. John wouldn't return her calls; Tamara had disappeared after lunch with no word as to her whereabouts. Security had come up, gone through her desk and purse, saying it was a requirement that had just been passed for every employee. Her face and knee were still bothering her, even though the bruises had faded quite a bit, and she was still hurting like hell inside over Mac and what she'd seen.

Obviously, it was over for Mac, because he hadn't tried calling her at all. What was it about relationships that prevented her from having and keeping a good one? Sighing, Sydney was ready to leave. She rose up from her desk and walked down the hall to the D.A.'s office to hand a file over to Caitlin, and wondered why the building was so quiet for five in the evening.

Usually people were running trying to finish their work before the end of the day. Frowning at that, she noticed Caitlin wasn't at her desk as she set the file down. "Caitlin?" she called, and heard someone rummaging around inside the office. Stepping to the side of the desk, she saw Lori coming out. "What are you doing?"

"Nothing, so get out of my way," Lori said, as she tried to push her way past Sydney.

Sydney stepped right in front of her, blocking Lori from leaving. "What were you doing in the D.A.'s office?"

"I said nothing, so get your fat ass out of my way."

Sydney blocked her again, noticing the file in her hand. "Did you take that?"

"So, what if I did?"

"Put it back, Lori; put it back now."

Lori laughed in her face. "I don't think so."

Sydney's eyes widened as realization set in. "You're the one. Things have been coming up missing for weeks. You've been taking them, haven't you? Haven't you, Lori?"

"So," she snorted. "What are you going to do? Nothing—that's what." Stepping up to Sydney, she snarled in her face. "Because if you tell anyone, I'll give you yours; besides, I still have to pay you back for tossing me in jail," she snapped.

They both turned their heads when the door opened, and Mac walked in.

Sydney smiled when she saw him; he was here to see her, and he could help her. "Mac, stop her; she's been stealing files from the D.A," Sydney said, listening as Lori laughed.

"You stupid bitch, who do you think I've been selling them to?" she gloated.

Sydney looked at Mac, her gaze wide when the stone façade came over his features, as he met her eyes. Her stomach dropped once everything started coming together. "You've been buying the things she's stolen from here?" she asked with confusion.

"Yes," he answered in a low voice.

Lori started laughing again. "Everything, from the cassette on the Chang case to the files and you; you are so stupid. Did you think he was seeing you because he liked you? He was screwing you to see what other information he could get out of you."

Sydney wrapped her arms around herself and met Mac's gaze.

"But nooooo, you're so freaking honest. My God, you're worthless, good for nothing, and stupid. Come on, Mac. Let's get out of here," she said, as she went to step around Sydney, only to be blocked again.

Sydney was not letting her get out of here; she'd deal with Mac later, but it pissed her off that she'd been used because of her job by both of them. No wonder everyone in the building clammed up in front of her, if they had an inkling of what Lori was doing. "You are not leaving this building with that file, Lori."

"Who's going to stop me, you?" She laughed and went to go past Sydney.

Adrenaline and anger surged through Sydney as she curled her hand into a fist, lifted her arm and punched Lori in the face, causing the file to drop and Lori to stumble back. When Lori came up, she had a knife in her hand and went after Sydney. Sydney threw her arms up to defend herself and heard Mac yelling "No!" as she felt the blade slicing her arm, sticking in her side. Sydney gasped, shock flooding her as she fell back, hitting the wall before sliding on the floor, her eyes going to the knife sticking out of her side as she grabbed her arm. The instinct to rip it out of her was overwhelming, but she listened to the voice in her head that yelled at her to leave it. Eyes wide with fear, she glanced up to see Mac throwing Lori against the wall, yelling for backup and an ambulance. Everything was getting hazy as she looked down to see blood covering her entire side, when she glimpsed Mac putting cuffs on Lori.

"You're under arrest for grand larceny and attempted murder," he was saying.

Sydney's eyes blurred. A cop, he was a cop.

"Sydney. Sydney, look at me," came a woman's voice.

Her eye's fluttered as she moved her head to see Tamara kneeling beside her, trying to stop the flow of blood.

"It's all right, it'll be all right; the ambulance is on the way."

Sydney glanced down to see her blood soaking through the material that Tamara had wrapped around her arm. She could feel the chaos erupting within the room. People started rushing by in a blur, as a dazed, dizzy feeling took over, and the pain of the knife decided to make itself known through her fogged mind.

"Mac, she's losing a lot of blood; I can't stop it," Tamara yelled, as she tried stopping the bleeding on her side around the blade, listening to Sydney whimper. "It's okay, Syd; it's going to be okay."

Through hazy eyes, Sydney glimpsed Mac yelling to an officer. "Where the hell is the ambulance?" he yelled as he knelt down beside her. "Sydney, God. Stay with us, honey. It's going to be all right," he said, as he took her hand, holding it above her head, mindful not to move her too much in case the blade moved as well.

"You- you thought I was helping her?" she whimpered, as she met his eyes.

"Don't talk, honey."

"You lied to me," she cried. "You just used me, like everyone else."

"Sydney, can you hear me?" another male voice asked.

She looked up to see not only John, but all of Mac's brothers.

"Zack, how is she?" Jake asked, kneeling beside them.

"They all knew, even John, and he let them use me. Zack, Jake called him Zack—brothers, all cops. Zack Mac Cloud, Detective Zackary Mac Cloud with the special undercover unit. Sydney raised her eyes to Mac. "You..." she slurred.

"Save your strength, honey," Mac said as he looked down at her, his face a collage of emotions as he held the bloodied makeshift bandages to her, trying to stop the flow with pressure.

"I-I was a-case to you," she said, her eyes fluttering as Mac ordered her to keep her eyes open and stay with them.

~~*~~

Sydney woke up to the sight of a hospital room and John leaning over her; immediately she started tearing up.

"Syd. Christ, Cuz, you are freaking lucky. How are you feeling? Lori didn't hit anything major, but damn! You bled like a stuck pig; scared the living shit out of me, let me tell you." Running a hand through his hair as he blew out a deep breath, he turned, noticing that she just lay there, letting her eyes follow him.

"You knew," her voice croaked and she watched him nod. "You let them use me; you knew."

"I couldn't say anything to you, Syd."

"How could you think I would do something like

that?" she cried. "That I'd steal important case information; didn't you stick up for me?"

"Yes, I did. I did, Syd, but when it went to special investigations my hands were tied."

Sydney snorted. "Special investigations, you mean Detective Zackary Mac Cloud." She winced as her hand moved to hold her side where the knife had been.

"You know?"

"Yeah, but it came a little too late, like me lying on the floor bleeding and hearing his brothers call him by name." Her voice rose with each word. She watched as his eyebrows went up and his shoulders tensed.

"Sydney, we had no choice. We had to clear you to make sure nothing could come back on you."

"Clear me? Yeah, he cleared me all right, right onto my damn back! When did it start?" she asked, her nostrils flaring and chest heaving, as she stared at the one person she thought she could trust the most.

"The day you met Zack; it was all set up by Tamara." He cringed as she looked straight at him.

Cold tingles raced through her brain. "The guy with the knife?"

"Tamara's nephew."

"She set it up?" Her head tipped down as she glanced up at him past lowered lashes, the ache in her heart mixing with the pain that so recently reared their heads.

"She had no choice; the D.A. called her in on it the day Lori swiped the tape."

Sydney closed her eyes. "Get out."

"What?"

"I said, get out!" Sydney yelled, wincing with the pain streaking through her side.

"Syd?"

"You no-good son of a bitch, I don't give a rat's ass what your fucking job is. I'm family! How could you even think I'd do something like that? I trusted you, John; you're the only family I have, and you screwed me! Get out and stay away from me!"

"Sydney?"

"What's all this yelling about?" the nurse asked as she rushed in. "Everyone on this end can hear you."

"Good, then all the back-stabbing bastards know I want nothing to do with any of them, especially the one who tossed me on my back just to get information for his fucking case! Get him out, get him out of here now!" She cried, as she grabbed her heaving side, darkness swirling as pain streaked through her battered body.

"Sir, you're going to have to leave."

"Sydney?" he asked, backing up as the nurse ushered him to the door.

"Get out and tell your friends to stay the hell away from me!" she cried, burying her head in the pillow as she sobbed.

~~*~~

Sydney looked up when the door opened, and a doctor walked in.

"Well Ms. Ripley, you are one lucky lady. The knife was deflected when the blade sliced your forearm before entering your side; it slid right between your tissue, not hitting bone or anything vital."

"That's good," she whispered.

"Very good. There's quite a line of cops, two D.A.'s, along with one secretary and a bartender with two biker guys who want to see you," he replied, as he walked over to her bedside, checking the stitches on her arm and wrapping it back up again. "Should I send them in?" he asked as he checked her side.

"No. I don't want to see anyone," Sydney whispered.

"So I heard earlier; I'm thinking you're calm now and a sedative isn't necessary?" he asked, as she shot a narrow-eyed look his way. "Right, are you sure? Because there's this one big detective, I think he said, who wants to get in here."

"I don't want to see any of them, particularly him."

"And what do you suggest I do with all of them?"

"Send them home."

"You're sure?"

"Yes."

"All right, but if they start an uprising I have no idea who I'm going to call, because the big guy's already growled and snapped at people, scaring them away," he said, as he walked out the door, shutting it behind him.

Sydney could hear the doctor relaying her wishes through the closed door; there were several mumbled responses and a loud one. Her chest tightened when she heard his voice complaining about not being allowed in, and as her eyes fluttered shut, tears escaped to slide down her cheek as she fell to sleep.

~~*~~

Mac walked up the hall, keeping to the side as the duty nurse left her desk to go check something. Keeping an eye out for the old badger, he walked right into Sydney's room, closing the door behind him. The room was dark except for a soft light shining as he spotted her outlined form lying on the bed. Quietly, he walked over to her and watched as she slept. He didn't know how long he stood there as his eyes moved over the visible bruises from her attack and the ones from her own sister. God, he had no idea what she must be going through; her own sister not only took advantage of her through her job, but tried to kill her.

He loved his brothers and didn't have a clue what he'd do if one of them turned on him like that. He couldn't blame her for being pissed at him; he knew it would happen. He may not show it to others, but he hurt. Never had a job been such an emotional drain on him, never had a woman taken ahold of him like this. His stone face dropped into anguish as he reached for her hand, turning when the door opened, his features changing back to the stone façade he always wore as he stepped to the door.

"You shouldn't be in there; Miss Ripley doesn't want any visitors," the old badger whispered when she had him in the hallway.

"I know. I just wanted to check on her."

"See that it doesn't happen again," she said, and turned into Sydney's room, shutting the door on him.

~~*~~

Sydney sat up with a wince as the doctor walked in.

"How are you feeling today?"

"Fine. Can I go home? I've been here a week."

"Yes, but there is something we should talk about first," he said, as he stood at the edge of her bed.

"What?"

"I wanted to assure you, that there should be no side effects from your trauma to the baby, you're still early

3

enough in your pregnancy and nothing was damaged from the attack."

Sydney's eyes widened. "What?"

"You should still meet with your ob-gyn and let them know what happened." He smiled. "But you and the baby should be fine."

"I I'm what- baby?"

"Yes, you're pregnant."

Sydney stared at him in shock. "You're sure?" she asked, as her heart pounded against her chest.

"Positive. We ran one before taking x-rays due to you being of child-bearing age. You didn't know?"

"No."

"I'm sorry, I thought you were aware. Is there someone you'd like me to call to take you home?"

"Uh, no. No, just call a cab, please."

"But you have no clothes; they cut them off in the E.R."

"What about a pair of um, hospital pants? I'll bring them back," she said as he rose off the bed.

"You're sure about not calling anyone?" he asked.

"Yes."

"Okay, I'll get rid of the line out there and be back with those bottoms."

"You didn't tell anyone, did you?"

"No, doctor-patient privilege, and neither you nor the baby was in any danger, requiring extreme actions to where we'd need to inform your next of kin."

"That's good, seeing as how my next of kin put me here," she snorted.

"Yes, I heard that," he replied as he walked out the door.

Her sarcastic look faded as soon as he left. Why she bothered to try and have a tough face when she was breaking down inside, she had no idea. Yes, she did. Tears flooded her eyes. It was because she had no one to lean on to be tough for her; all she had was herself. Sliding her good hand over her abdomen, she felt the tears marking her cheeks. Well not just her—anymore.

Glancing up as the door opened, Sydney went to ask the doctor a question and instead she saw Beth, Ma... Zack's mom come in with the hospital pants. Her heart jumped against her chest at the thought of having to see any one of them.

"I hear you're leaving today," she said, as she walked over to the bedside.

"I would appreciate it if you left, please."

"Yes, I've heard something about no visitors, but you see that doesn't include me," Beth said with a smile as Sydney's eyes followed her. "And don't worry, I sent all the uniforms home; no one here but us girls." She patted Sydney's leg. "Come on, let's get you dressed and I'll take you home."

"Thank you, but I'd rather you leave."

"Sydney, there's nothing wrong with letting me help you."

"You knew what was going on just like everyone else, just like my own cousin, and you all let me be used," her voice cracked with anguish as her eyes burned with tears. "You don't have to pretend anymore, Beth. You don't have to be nice to me; I was just a case."

"They were doing their job, Sydney; you can't blame them for that."

"Yes, I can," she cried as the tears flowed down her

face. "Because he turned it into something more when he knew it would end, and everyone went right along with him, not giving a damn as to how I would feel."

Beth was silent as Sydney covered her face with her hands and cried. Lifting a hand, she rubbed Sydney's back. "Sydney, Zack's upset by what happened. When you're a cop you can't let your emotions get in the way of your job, but he did and he's worried sick about you. Do you know how hard it was for him to keep doing his job with the feelings he has for you?"

"Oh yeah, they run deep. That's why he was necking on a blonde the other night."

"She was a cop, Sydney. It was set up to make you think that way, because he knew he was getting too close to you."

"Maybe he should have thought about that before he slept with me," she snapped. Anger riding on top of hurt was a powerful emotion and she stopped before she said something that she'd never be able to take back. "Is there anyone on the force that doesn't know?"

"Sydney…"

"Please leave."

Beth looked at her for a moment before tipping her head in response, as she rose off the bed. "Are you sure you don't want a ride home?"

"Yes."

"Sydney please let me…"

"Beth, I'd rather not be made a fool of any more, thank you. Please leave," she said, wiping the tears away as Beth walked out of the room.

Breathing deeply, she let it out slowly, her mind twirling with every kind of emotion as her body and soul ached. Swinging her legs off the side of the bed, Sydney put the hospital pants on. Having the use of one hand and a stitched-up side wasn't the easiest to work with. Glancing up when the door opened again, she hoped like hell it wasn't anyone else she didn't want to see.

The nurse smiled at her. "I called the cab," she said, as she helped Sydney finish getting dressed, and then opened the closet to retrieve her purse, handing it to her as another nurse brought a wheelchair in.

CHAPTER 14

SYDNEY SAT ON HER couch trying to figure out what she was going to do. The phone was driving her crazy; it wouldn't stop ringing. Well, it might if she picked it up and talked to whoever was calling. She'd been sitting there for two hours when there was a knock at her door. Lifting her head, she stared at it as though the door could tell her who was there. They knocked again.

"Sydney, I know you're home," came a masculine voice.

Ma...no it's Zack, she thought, as she sat there staring at the door.

"Open the door, Sydney."

She could feel the tears sliding down her cheeks and buried her head on the pillow between her bent-up knees.

"Sydney, I can hear you crying. Open the door, honey," he said. "Sydney, I'll break the door open," he said. When she didn't answer, he took out his lock picks.

Sydney turned her head when she heard the door open. She jumped off the couch as fast as she could, which wasn't quick, as he walked in, shutting the door behind him. "Get out."

"Sydney, I just want to talk," Mac said, as he turned to her, noticing the way she favored her hurt side as she pressed a hand against it.

"I don't want to talk to you. Get out," she said, as she picked up the phone dialing the police station. "This is 2424 Grayson, I need Officer John Monroe's patrol car here; someone is refusing to leave my residence," she said, and backed up when Mac took the phone away from her.

"This is Detective Zack Mac Cloud, badge number five fifty-four; everything's all set," he said, his gaze finding hers as he hit the off button.

Sydney looked at him with tear-glazed eyes. "I want you to leave now."

"I'm not leaving until we talk," he said, as she turned her back to him. "Sydney, I'm sorry. I never meant to hurt you; that was the last thing on my mind. I had to find out if you were helping Lori; I had a job to do. I never planned on caring about you. It was supposed to be a quick job, in and out, get the information, no feelings involved. But things changed, Sydney, I..." Mac stopped and turned when the door opened.

"I got a call on the radio," John said, as he and Barney walked in the door.

Sydney turned around. "I want him to leave," she said and then walked to her bedroom, shutting and locking the door.

"What happened?" John asked as Mac turned around to face him.

"She wouldn't let me in, so I picked the lock."

John's eyebrows shot up. "You B & E'd?"

"I could hear her crying and I needed to talk to her."

"Did you?"

"I tried," Mac said and ran a hand through his hair.

"Maybe you should give it a few more days," John suggested.

"Yeah, maybe." He turned to look at the closed door before turning on his heel and leaving.

"Syd, he's gone," John said through the bedroom door.

"Good, you can leave too." She listened to him walk away from her door and shut the outside one. Getting up, she walked in to the living room and locked the door. Then she went back to the bedroom and crawled into bed, hugging her pillow to her as the tears continued to flow.

~~*~~

Two days later, Sydney parked in front of the courthouse, getting out of her car. She could feel people staring at her as she walked back to her desk, and saw a secretary from one of the other offices sitting behind it.

"Sydney, how are you?" the older lady asked.

"Fine, thank you. I just came to pick up my things," she answered, as she picked up the family pictures off her desk and put them into the shoulder bag she was carrying.

"Your things?" she asked looking confused.

"Yes." Sydney turned and walked toward Tamara's office, knocking on the open door before going in.

"Sydney, I've been worried about you. You haven't called; how are you?"

"I'm fine, Tamara. I came to give you this." She handed over a piece of folded paper.

Tamara took it and opened it up. After reading it, she set it aside and looked up at Sydney. "I won't accept this."

"You have no choice," Sydney said.

"Sydney, think about what you're doing; you're the best secretary I've ever had. Are you going to throw everything away because of an investigation?"

"Yeah, that's why you went right along with them. I have

thought about it, Tam. I can not stay employed somewhere when they thought I was involved in a crime. Everyone here, everyone in this building knew what was going on, and all of you jumped on the bandwagon to help them make a fool of me," she said, as her heart battered her chest. She'd known something would be said and hated that it had, because now she had to talk about it and bring the hurt to the surface all over again. "You had your nephew pretend to try and assault me, that day I met Ma...Zack, so I'd fall into right into Mac's arms. Damn, I don't even know what to call him anymore," she cried, as she felt her eyes burning. "I'm sorry, but I can't stay here, not with everyone staring at me every time I walk down the hall, wondering if I might have had something to do with it." She was starting to get upset, tears glistening in her eyes. "I won't have people talking behind my back, when...when..."

"When what?" Tamara asked concerned.

"When my baby is born," Sydney cried, as she lifted her hands to cover her nose and mouth.

"Baby?" Tamara asked shocked. "You're pregnant?"

"Yes. Obviously, one of the condoms didn't work," she cried. "Don't you dare call him, Tam. Do you hear me? Don't you call him about this," she cried, as she turned, running out of the office.

When she hit the steps, she saw Mac leaning on her car, and she turned down the sidewalk. When she heard him call her name, she started running and ducked into the mom and pop store she always stopped at.

The clerk looked up at her. "Sydney, what's wrong?"

"Can I use your back door?" she asked.

"Yeah, yeah," he said, and took her to the back. "Do you need me to call the cops?"

"No," she said, as he opened the door and she went out into the alleyway. She ran behind four buildings and then went up another alleyway and peered around the corner. Her side was killing her, but she'd be damned if he caught up with her right now. She saw him going into the mom and pop store, and she came out of the alley, running to her car, hopped in it and took off in the other direction. Stopping at a red light, she took her glasses off to wipe her eyes so she could see where she was going. When the light turned green she took off, not caring what direction she was driving.

Mac pulled his phone out and called the station. "John, have you seen Sydney?"

"No, not since she threw us both out. Why?"

"Because she just gave me the slip; I was waiting for her at the courthouse and when she came out, she started running."

"Leave it to my cousin to give one of the great Mac Clouds the slip."

"This isn't funny, Monroe!"

"I know; listen, if I see her I'll let you know."

"Fine," Mac said and hit the end button. Blowing out a frustrated breath, he headed back toward the station. God, he wanted her, just wanted to talk to her, hold her, tell her everything was going to be all right. Stopping, Mac stared at the road in front of him, unseeing as his feelings for her hit him. And with a smile, he went on his way.

Sydney ended up at the spot Mac- Zack had taken her to watch the sun set. She put the car in park and sat there, watched the sun set and cried. Taking her glasses off, she reached into her bag for tissue and tried to get them to stop. Several hours after the sunset, she was still sitting there staring out at the night sky with sore red eyes, still trying to figure out what to do. She knew she wanted the baby, but should she tell him or not? That was the question she couldn't answer. Not after he lied to her, let her believe he cared for her. But he told her he cared for her two nights ago when he broke into her apartment; was that just to ease his guilty conscience or did he mean it? Sliding her hand to her stomach, she wished she knew what to do. Starting the car, she headed back home.

When she got home, Tamara was waiting for her. "Well, it's about time you got home. I've been waiting for hours."

"What do you want, Tam?" she asked as she got out of her car.

"I wanted to make sure you're all right. After all, you did give a Mac Cloud the slip, which I will say was very interesting to watch from my window. But I must say I can't accept this," she said, taking Sydney's resignation letter out and tearing it up. "For one, you know we need everything in triplicate and for another, I am not letting you leave. Think about it Sydney, where are you going to go and find a job with a baby on the way?"

"I'm tired, Tam, and don't want to talk about it."

"Are you going to tell him?" Tam asked as Sydney tensed.

"You're not, are you? Sydney, every child deserves to know their father."

"I-I don't know what I'm going to do. I think and think, but I still come up with blanks. I know I should tell him, but I-I'm scared to." She couldn't hold it in anymore and broke down, all her fears and emotions hitting the surface like a cresting wave. "I don't know if he slept with me because it was easier for him to do his job, or if he did it because he wanted me."

Tamara wrapped her arm around Sydney's shoulders and walked her to the door. "Let's go inside," she said as she took the keys out of Sydney's hand and opened the door, shutting it behind them.

"I just don't know what to do," Sydney said, as she sat in her couch.

"Why don't you talk to him?" Tamara sat down next to her.

"I can't, he hurt me."

"Sydney, he cares for you. He went berserk when you passed out in the hallway, scowling at everyone. It took two of his brothers to get him out of the way so the EMT's could get to you, and then he started on them because they took so long getting there. I thought the doctor was going to call in the National Guard when you refused to see visitors. It took all three of his brothers to pull him out of the hospital."

"But he lied to me."

"How? Did you come straight out and ask him if he was a cop? If you did and he said no, he was justified under the law to do so. Did you ask him if he was undercover, or what Lori was trying to sell in the bar? He didn't lie to you, Sydney, because you never asked, and from what you told me he told you straight out that there were some things he couldn't tell you just yet. Sydney, I'm not saying that you have to tell him about the baby right away, but you do have to tell him. You know it's the right thing to do."

"I know."

"Do you want me to help you get ready for bed?" she asked, and Sydney shook her head.

"All right, I'll leave you alone for now. You know you're my friend and not just a secretary. Call me tomorrow and let me know how you're doing."

She rose off the couch. "Tam, tell him when I'm ready to talk that I'll come to him."

"Sure, Sydney. Try to get some sleep," she said, as she headed for the door and shut it on her way out.

Sydney sat back down, digesting what Tamara had said. It was true. She had never come straight out and asked, except for the Chang thing and he had told her the truth on that. Letting out a heavy sigh, she got up from the couch and locked the door before going to bed.

~~*~~

"Zack, its Tam; I just left Sydney's house. She's fine. She wanted me to tell you that she'll come find you when she's ready to talk...I don't know...don't be pushy with me, Mac Cloud. Give it a couple of days...all right, bye." Hitting the end button on her cell phone, Tamara shook her head. "Men," she said to herself as she turned the car heading for her condo. She was at a stoplight when she heard a bike pull up alongside of her. Looking over, she saw Detective Gabriel Mac Cloud smiling at her. "Do all the Mac Clouds own loud noisy bikes?"

Gabe grinned. "Family trait. Want a ride?"

Tam's pussy clenched when his cheek dimpled. "Really, Detective. Do you think I'd get on one of those?" she asked, as he shrugged a shoulder.

"You could have fun, Tam."

"I don't have fun with playboys," Tamara said, smiling at him.

"And who said I was a playboy?"

"The women of the entire force for one, and that smile of yours runs a close second."

"You like my smile?" he asked, his lips turning up in a satisfied masculine grin.

"I plead the fifth, Detective," she said, taking off when the light turned green.

Gabe was still smiling when he started his bike moving. She was one hot-looking lady. He'd told her so the first time they met two years ago, and she had the gall to tell him to keep it in his pants, because he wouldn't get anywhere except cut off if he played games with her.

Hell, at least she was flirting with him; it had taken him a year and a half to get this far with her. But she had one thing wrong—he flirted, yeah. But he hadn't been with a woman in over a year and he knew damn well she hadn't been with a guy either in that amount of time. Well, her time was running out and he was Father Time. Gabe turned heading for the Mer-Fay. He needed a drink and a talk with his brother. Parking the bike, he walked into the bar and headed straight for Zack.

CHAPTER 15

"HEY, MAN."

Mac looked up at his brother. "What are you up to?"

"Besides flirting with Tamara at the stoplight?" he asked with a smile. "She likes my smile."

"She said that?"

"No, she decided to plead the fifth."

Mac snorted. "Now that I believe."

"I know she was waiting at Sydney's, and they talked for a while outside before going in."

"Did you hear anything?" Mac asked as he glanced over, gaze narrowing when his brother said nothing, as he twirled his keys between his hands. "Gabe?"

"Yeah, I heard some of the conversation."

Mac raised an eyebrow. "What did you hear?"

"Walt, get me a beer, will you?" he asked, waiting as he took a couple of gulps before looking at his older brother again. "Okay, Sydney was upset because she doesn't know if you slept with her for the job or because you care for her; she's scared and confused. Tam tore up her resignation letter and told her to forget it."

"What's she scared about?" he asked, knowing his brother was keeping something from him.

Taking a deep breath, Gabe turned to face him.

"Because she's hurting, and she's not sure how to tell you she's pregnant."

"Pregnant?" Eyes wide, Mac stared at him. "Are you sure you heard that right?"

"Yes, I'm sure," he answered, as he raked a hand through his hair. "Zack, you better not say a word that you found out from me."

"Sydney's pregnant," he said, sitting there for a minute before getting up.

Walt grabbed ahold of his arm. "Tam told you that Sydney would come to you when she wanted to talk."

"That was before I found out she's pregnant."

"Zack, if she told Tam to pass that message on to you, then she had some luck in talking to her. If you go busting into her house again, you might undo what is done. Now, sit down and stay away from her until she comes to you."

Gabe nodded. "Walt's right, man. The last time you tried bullying her to talk, she called the police and then ran from you. Give her a few days."

Mac sat back down on the bar stool, taking several gulps of his beer. "I'm going to be a father," he said and then looked up at his brother. "Woo-hoo, I'm going to be a father!" he yelled. "Round on me." He grinned, pulling his brother into a hug as Greeley and the others cheered, and that was another thing she was going to kill him over when she found out. Greeley, Brian, and ninety-five percent of the guys that hung out here were undercovers like him, needing a place to go they could trust that wouldn't blow that cover. That's why his Uncle Walt had opened the bar in the first place, before handing it over to him.

Zack

~~*~~

Two days later Sydney went back to work. Tamara had told her that she and Gladys, the lady who covered for her, kept the resignation thing to themselves. Sydney was already a month pregnant and she could feel it. Morning sickness had hit her well and hard this morning with the smell of coffee almost doing her in.

"What's that?" Tam asked, as she walked by Sydney's desk.

"It's orange sherbet ice cream mixed with lemon-lime soda."

"Is it good?"

"Yeah, and the thing I seem able to keep down."

"Ah, the first trimester. I remember when my sister went through that; how are the wounds doing?"

"Good, the stitches come out on Friday."

"Have you thought anymore about talking to Zack?"

"Yes," was all she said, and Tamara nodded.

"If you need anything, let me know."

"I will."

"Why don't you take Friday off; you know how it is going to the doctor's office."

"Thanks," Sydney replied, as Tamara walked back to her office.

~~*~~

Sydney walked out of the doctor's office and headed for the courthouse. Walking in, she smiled at the lady sitting at her desk. "Is Tamara in?"

"Yes. Sydney, I'm glad you decided to come back."

"Thanks, Gladys, me too," she said, walking to Tamara's office.

"Hey, how's wounded woman doing?" Tamara asked as Sydney stepped into her office.

"Good," she answered as she held her arm up. "They told me to keep this arm brace on for a few weeks, until I go back again, and they wrapped my side; I'm not to do anything strenuous, like rock climbing or mountain biking for a couple of weeks." She smiled.

"Crap, so plane jumping is out this weekend?" Tam grinned.

Sydney held her side as she tried not to laugh. "Ooh, it hurts. Don't make me laugh."

"Sorry about that. So, what are you doing here? I figured you'd have better things to do on a day off than spend it at the office," Tamara said smiling.

"Like you should talk, Miss 'I'm here twenty-four seven'."

"Hey, I have no life, what can I say?"

"You would if Gabe had anything to do about it."

"Ah, yes. Mr. Hot Shot Mac Cloud, playboy of the precinct."

"Actually, from what I heard, he's not. He was flirtatious, but left alone, at Mitch's wedding, even though one of the bridesmaids so wanted to go home with him."

"I'll keep that in mind; so, tell me, Sydney. Why are you here?"

"I was wondering if you know where Mac Zack might be."

"Last I heard he was down at the station; that was about two hours ago, but he may still be there. The boys brought in someone they were interrogating."

"Thanks," Sydney said and turned to leave.

"Does this mean you're going to tell him?"

"This means that I'm going to talk with him and I'll see from there."

"Good luck, Sydney."

"Thanks again," she said, smiling as she walked out of the courthouse and down the Sidewalk, heading for the police station.

Her nostrils flared, chest lifted with the deepness of the breath she took, glancing at the door she breathed out through her mouth, taking a hold of the handle, she walked through the door to the reception desk, taking another deep breath as the officer looked up.

"May I help you?" he asked.

Sydney smiled as she tried to control her racing heart. "Yes, is Detective Mac Cloud still here?" she asked, watching as the Sergeant looked at her like she'd lost her mind.

"Lady, I've got three of them here, any particular one you're looking for?"

"Oh I-I'm sorry," she stumbled. "Mac, ah Zack," Sydney said breathlessly as he picked up the phone.

"Is Zack Mac Cloud at his desk? I have someone out here who wants to see him. Hold on…" He held the phone down and looked at her. "What's your name?" he asked.

"Sydney, Sydney Ripley," she said, as he put the phone back to his mouth.

"Sydney Ripley, all right, yeah. They said he's still in interrogation, but you can go back and wait at his desk."

"Did they say how long he'd be in there?"

"One never knows; do you want to go back or not?" he asked as she nodded her head. "All right, come with me." He buzzed open the door to let her through.

Sydney followed him down a hallway, up an elevator

to the third floor and into a large room filled with desks. Glancing around, she saw several people look her way. She moved her eyes to the sergeants' back, keeping them on him until he stopped near the back of the room.

"This is his desk; you can sit here."

"Thank you," she said, as she sat on one of the chairs against the wall.

~~*~~

"Are we done here, Detective? My client would like to go home sometime today."

Being the lead detective on the case, Mac leaned over the table, meeting the lawyers gaze. "We have a few more questions, counselor. Might as well get them out of the way instead of having to pull him in again, but then again, that is your choice," he stated calmly, his eyebrow lifting as the attorney nodded his head. Straightening up, he turned to Gabe so he could take over. They ended up questioning him for over an hour by the time Mac said that they were finished for the day. Running a hand through his hair, Mac sighed as he watched them leave.

"He's going to be a hard nut to crack," Jake said, coming up beside him.

"Yeah, but he'll crack," Gabe said from behind them.

"Mac Cloud," a female voice called out.

"Yeah?"

They all turned at the same time.

"Sorry, I keep forgetting there's more than one of you," a female officer said.

"It's all right, Clair. What's up?" Jake asked.

"Zack, there's a lady here waiting to see you; she's been sitting by your desk for about two hours."

Mac frowned. "A lady? Any name?"

"No, but I think I've seen her working at the court-house," she replied, jumping out of the way as he flew by her.

Mac slid around the corner, and kept on running, causing everyone to look at him and smile. When he could see his desk in the corner, he slowed down. Sydney was sitting beside the desk, her head between her hands with her elbows resting on her knees. Slowing down, he walked the last five feet until he stood in front of her and knelt down when she didn't look up. Tipping his head to see her face, he saw her eyes were closed. Smiling, he lightly placed his hands on her knees. "Honey, wake up," he said and listened to her mumble something. "Honey," he said a little louder, watching as her eyes fluttered as she sat up.

"Sorry, I think I fell asleep," she said, and saw his smile as her sight cleared from sleep.

"I'm the one who's sorry; no one told me you were out here."

"They said you were interrogating someone."

"Yeah, but Jake and Gabe could have finished without me," he said, as he brought a hand up to brush some of her hair aside. "Since when do you fall asleep in the middle of the day?" he asked, watching her as he waited for her answer.

"Just lately," She replied without looking at him.

"Tam said that when you were ready to talk you'd come to me. Are you ready?" he asked and as she nodded, she turned her gaze to look at him. Her eyes started tearing up, his hands caressing her knees in an attempt to comfort her.

"You hurt me," she said.

"I never meant to."

"Did you sleep with me for me or the job?"

"For you, well, and me," he said with a smile causing her to chuckle. "Sydney, I…" he started, but she cut him off.

"What is that smell?" she asked, wrinkling her nose up.

"Hey Zack, dinner's here," Jake said, carrying two Styrofoam take-out plates to their desks.

"Oh God," Sydney groaned, her hand flying to her mouth, causing both of them to look at her. "Bathroom." She gagged behind her hand, causing Mac to jump up, take her hand, and run. People got out of the way as they went down a hall. When he pushed a door open, she ran in and he was right behind her until a female called out.

"Mac Cloud, you can't come in here."

"Watch me," he said as he found the stall Sydney was in. Kneeling on the floor next to her, he held her hair out of the way, rubbed her back with his other hand as she emptied the contents of her stomach into the toilet.

Gabe shut the ladies' room door, giving them some privacy as he and Jake stood guard in front of it.

Sydney felt drained. She sat back on her heels, taking the toilet paper Mac handed her to wipe her mouth.

"Are you okay, honey?" Mac asked, kneeling behind her he watched her nod. "Is it all right to move you?" he asked, his hand moving in slow circles around her back.

"Yeah, I think so," she answered, as she rose to her feet with his help.

Mac led her over to the sink and turned on the cold water, where she washed her mouth out and then splashed some on her face. Turning, he grabbed some paper towels, handing them to her, and shut the water off as she wiped off her face and mouth. After she threw the paper towel away, Mac lifted her to sit on the counter. Coming to stand between her legs, he brought his hands up, cupping her face. "Are you all right?" he asked.

"Yes, as long as I don't move around too much."

"Sydney, I never meant to hurt you; I'd cut off my left arm before I'd see you hurt."

"What about the right one?"

His lips turned up with a smile as the corner of his eyes crinkled. "You must be feeling better; your sense of humor is breaking out. But yes, I'd give my right one too, and then you'd have to spoon feed me. Sydney, I love you, honey," he said, as her eyes started tearing up again, and then she was crying and gasping for air at the same time.

CHAPTER 16

"WHAT IN THE HELL is going on out here?" Captain Kline asked, pushing his way through the crowd that had gathered outside of the ladies' bathroom.

"It's Mac Cloud, sir. He's holding up the bathroom," came a female voice.

"It must be Zack seeing as how these two are out here and Mitch is gone," he said walking up to the front. "What's he doing in the ladies' room?"

Jake and Gabe glanced at each other. "Sydney got sick; he's helping her," Jake answered.

"Sydney, that little girl who works at the courthouse we just cleared?"

"Yes sir," Gabe answered.

"She the reason he's been a bear of an asshole since that case ended?"

"Yes sir," Jake answered.

"She here to put him back to the regular ass we love and know so well?"

"Yes sir," They both answered.

"And how is she going to do that?" Kline asked.

"Probably by telling him she's pregnant," Gabe said causing Jake's head to whip around to look at him.

"She's pregnant?" Jake said.

"Yep, but she doesn't know, he knows, so no one's going to say anything until he does," Gabe threatened as he looked at the faces in the hall way.

"Well then, this is a must see. Anyone have some popcorn?" the Captain asked and was handed a bag of microwavable popcorn.

~~*~~

"Sydney, calm down, honey. Take deep breaths. Let them out slowly. I think you're hyperventilating," Mac said as he held her.

"Y-you l-love me?" Sydney asked against his shoulder.

Mac pulled back, cupping his hands around her face. "With my entire heart, honey." His head lowered to press his lips against hers. "With my entire heart."

Sydney pulled back. "Mac-, Zack-, damn, I don't even know what to call you."

"Either one, honey," he said, wiping her tears away with the pads of his thumbs.

"I came here to talk, but I also came to tell you something," she said, as she raised her gaze to his.

"What do you want to tell me, honey?" he asked, looking at her as he lowered his hands to her waist.

"When I was brought to the E.R. they had to run some tests, and found something out," she said, as she took in a shuddering breath, trying to calm herself. "One of the nights that we made love, the- the condom didn't work. I'm- I'm pregnant."

"You're pregnant?" he asked, as she nodded.

"Please don't be mad at me. I had to find out how you felt about me before I told you."

Taking a deep breath, she figured she'd best just come

clean with him, so she never had to feel bad about anything again. "I didn't want to tell you about the baby at first. I was afraid, afraid that you slept with m-me just because of the c-case." Stopping for a moment to breathe deeply, his fingers and hands caressed her from her back to her arms and thighs. "I'm not sure if you want a baby; we haven't known each other that long and then everything fell apart, and now you say you love me. I think I needed to hear that first, so it won't always be at the back of my mind if you were just with me because of the baby," she said, tears flowing from her eyes as she watched a soft smile come over his face.

"I'm going to be a daddy," he said, his lips meeting hers in a sensual, loving kiss. "I love you, Sydney."

Sydney cried out as she wrapped her arms around his neck. "I love you too, Mac. I love you so much," she mumbled, as she buried her face into the crook of his neck, breathing in his scent as his arms wrapped around her, holding her close. She cried with the sheer joy she felt.

~~*~~

"Hey, I have to go to the bathroom. Move," came a female voice.

"Sorry Jordan, you'll either have to wait or use the men's room," Cap said.

"Why, what's going on?"

"Zack's being told he's going to be a daddy." Cap grinned, looking at her.

"No shit. Well, hand me that popcorn, sir," she said, taking a handful.

"Thought you had to go the bathroom," Cap said, looking at her.

"Are you kidding? Do you think I'd miss seeing another one of the great Mac Clouds being taken down by a woman? Hey, where's the chocolate?" she asked and smiled at both of the brothers. "So, which one of you is next?" she asked. Everyone laughed as they pointed to each other.

~~*~~

Mac kissed her again and then brought his head up. "Sydney Ripley, will you do me the honor of becoming my wife?" he asked, pulling a one-carat diamond engagement ring out of his pocket, sliding it onto her finger.

"Yes, Zackary Mac Cloud. I would love to be your wife," she answered, smiling as his lips pressed against hers. Leaning back, she said, "What are we going to do about living space?

We can't bring a baby to live above a bar and my apartment has the one room."

"Good question," he replied. "I did see this house for sale three blocks from my mom's."

"Really?"

"Yep, has three bedrooms with a master bedroom, bath, and a den. It even has a fireplace in the living room." He said smiling back at her.

"Checked it out, have you?"

"You could say that," he said, as he leaned in for another kiss. "But I think we better go home."

"Why, Mac? Are you horny?" she asked with a big smile.

"Why, yes, I am. But I think we have a crowd outside and that, my sweet, is the one thing keeping me from taking you here and now," he said, with a devilish smile, as he gathered her up into his arms, stepping toward the door. "Gabe, open the door," he hollered and watched as the door swung open.

When they stepped into the hallway they were met with smiling faces.

"So, does another Mac Cloud bite the dust of bachelorhood?" Jordan asked.

"Yes, Jordan, and I'm going to be a daddy." He grinned, holding Sydney tight to him as the crowd cheered.

"Just what I need, another generation of Mac Clouds under my supervision." Cap smiled as he slapped him on the back.

"You'll be Chief by then and won't bother with us peons," Mac said as they started walking down the hallway.

"Right, like I said, under my supervision."

"It could be a girl," Sydney said.

"Honey, the Mac Clouds run strongly with boys," Mac stated, as he leaned in to kiss her.

"Yes, but the Ripley's run toward girls," she answered, kissing him back.

"Whatever it is, I'll love it all the same." He smiled, wishing for it to be a little girl.

ABOUT THE AUTHOR

Ms. Salo, is a current member of RWA and reached RWA's PRO status in April of 2015.

Ms. Salo, is serving as the Vice President of Communications for the 2018-19 term, and served as the Interim Vice President of Programs for her RWA chapter, The Sunshine State Romance Authors for the 2017 year.

C.A. is originally from north central Massachusetts, and moved down to central Florida where she swears she hates shoveling as much as humidity.

C and her Hubs tied the knot during an intimate ceremony on her Grandmother's birthday in March at a beautiful and charming B & B in Fl.

Blog: http://authorcasalo.blogspot.com/
Facebook: https://www.facebook.com/authorcasalo
Twitter: https://twitter.com/AuthorCASalo
Website: www.authorcasalo.com

www.ingramcontent.com/pod-product-compliance
Lightning Source LLC
Chambersburg PA
CBHW071914220626
47052CB00002B/344